ORPHANS OF GUNSWIFT GRAZE

OTHER FIVE STAR WESTERN TITLES BY L. P. HOLMES:

River Range (2006)
Roaring Acres (2007)
Riders of the Coyote Moon (2009)
Singing Wires (2010)
Desert Steel (2010)

Orphans of Gunswift Graze

A WESTERN STORY

L. P. Holmes

FIVE STAR
A part of Gale, Cengage Learning

GALE
CENGAGE Learning®

Detroit • New York • San Francisco • New Haven, Conn • Waterville, Maine • London

LIBRARY OF CONGRESS CATALOGING-IN-PUBLICATION DATA

Holmes, L. P. (Llewellyn Perry), 1895–
    Orphans of gunswift graze : a western story / by L.P. Holmes.
    — 1st ed.
        p. cm.
    "A Five Star western."
    ISBN 978-1-4328-2562-1 (hardcover) — ISBN 1-4328-2562-3
(hardcover) 1. Ranchers—Fiction. 2. Pasture, Right of—Fiction. I.
Title.
PS3515.O4448O77 2012
813'.52—dc22   2011049907

First Edition. First Printing: May 2012.
Published in 2012 in conjunction with Golden West Literary Agency.

Printed in Mexico
1 2 3 4 5 6 7 16 15 14 13 12

ADDITIONAL COPYRIGHT INFORMATION

CHAPTER ONE

The stage rolled into Warm Creek at 2:04 P.M., four minutes off the hour, and Gil Lambie, the whip, with thirty-odd miles of sagebrush desert and plains road behind him, was justifiably upset over this fact. So it was with an unaccustomed flourish that Lambie, dour and brusque as he was, brought his sweating team of six and his weather-whipped old thorough-brace Concord to a wheel-clacking halt before the Starlight Hotel.

Up on the box beside Lambie, Dave Kerchival stretched, beat an accumulation of gray Nevada dust from a solid pair of flannel-clad shoulders, and spoke with dry humor.

"As a whip, Gil, you're a top hand. But as a gent to pass the time of day with, you're sure one frugal Siwash. You haven't swapped ten words with me all the way from Fort Devlin."

"Talk," retorted Lambie gruffly, "is plumb useless business and a criminal waste of breath unless you got something to say. Of which I ain't."

Kerchival chuckled. "That is what Mel Rhodes would call a gross understatement of fact, Gil."

He dug a limp gripsack from the luggage boot under the seat, tossed it to the ground, and followed it down, a tall man, long of leg, and with a saddle man's lean limberness about hip and flank. He had a brown, blunt-jawed face and a pair of rock-gray eyes that fed on surroundings that were familiar and good after an absence.

Why was it, he mused, that a man always expected some

7

change in things he'd been away from, even for a little time? Maybe it was because he instinctively resented change in anything that went to make up his chosen and familiar world and was always slightly fearful that some such change might creep up on him in the dead of night. Which was, conceded Kerchival, somewhat akin to the reasoning of a small boy, and his eyes crinkled slightly at the fancy.

But there had been no change here. This town of Warm Creek in early afternoon was no different than he'd seen it a hundred times before. The tawny run of the dusty street was the same, with the black-angled shadows beginning to build and spread on the east side of the buildings. There were some drowsing cow ponies and a couple of buckboards scattered along the hitch racks, and there was Sam Liederman's old Buster dog asleep on Sam's store porch. On the bench beside the door, a dumpy, round-bodied figure in the shade of the overhang, Jack Tully, smoked his pipe and watched the town.

Beyond the northern edge of town began the long lift of the Mount Cherokee plateau, to sweep vastly up and away through sun-drenched miles to timber-darkened crests. A little breeze, pressing down from these heights, sent dust curls dancing along the street and brought to a man's nostrils a dry, sweet fragrance of cedar and pine. Yeah, it was good to be back.

Kerchival caught up his gripsack and climbed the hotel steps. There he stopped, his pulse beginning to strum, as it always did when he looked at Lear Hendron. She had stepped from the hotel door and now came swiftly across the porch toward him. For one bright moment he knew the exultant thought that she was here especially to meet him, but this died swiftly as he glimpsed the pinch of anxiety in her eyes. Here, he realized soberly, was a girl who would never come running with warm eagerness to any man, least of all to him. For she was Abel Hendron's daughter and weighted with the cold, formal, unbending Hendron pride.

He touched his hat and said: "Lear, it's good to see you." He tried to keep his tone casual and matter-of-fact, but he saw that this didn't matter, either; this girl was concerned with something far apart from him. She did drop a hand on his arm, but it was only a gesture of urgency.

"Dave, you've got to get over to the Rialto right away. They've got Bill Yeager in there and they're putting the pressure on him."

"They . . . ?"

"The Ballards. Virg is with them. They've been drinking. Dusty Elliot brought the word, hoping Father had arrived. I came down from the ranch with Dusty in the buckboard. Father was to have followed a little later, to meet Bill Yeager here and have a talk with him. But Father hasn't shown up yet, and I'm afraid. You know how the Ballards are. . . ."

"Yeah," said Kerchival, a trifle harshly. "I know how the Ballards are. Same old argument with Bill Yeager, I suppose . . . trying to bully him into closing the Kingfisher Creek drive trail?"

Lear Hendron nodded a dark head. "Yes, that's it."

Looking down into the wide anxiety of her eyes, Dave Kerchival realized that this was one of the very few times that Lear Hendron had ever stood this close to him. Twice he had danced with her. That was before she had stopped going to the occasional soirées that women of the town held in Sam Liederman's warehouse.

There was so much about this girl that Kerchival could not understand. There was slim, striking beauty in her, and a full and eager life. He had seen her ride like the wind and heard her laugh with bright exultancy over the thrill of such action, as though for this brief time she had known momentary escape of some kind. Then the laughter would die and her mood turn still and distant and somehow brooding. And more and more during the past year this reserved and distant mood had held her.

Her mouth was soft and crimson, but beneath it was a chin molded to a dignity and pride that no man dared offend. Yet more than once Dave Kerchival had wondered recklessly what the reaction would be were a man to take her in his arms and savor those crimson lips. Would it awaken any other reaction but a cold and scathing anger?

She seemed to read that thought in him now, for she stiffened and her hand fell away from his arm.

"Don't look at me like that," she said almost sharply. "You heard what I told you. There could be trouble in the Rialto . . . trouble for Bill Yeager. Get over there!"

There was a bite in her tone that had the shock of cold water. Kerchival matched her now, mood for mood. "Where's Dusty?" he rapped bleakly.

"Trying to round up Joe Orchard, I think. It doesn't matter where he is. You're the man who can handle things over there."

"Some satisfaction there, to know I'm good for something," said Kerchival, tossing down his gripsack and turning away.

There was anger in his stride as he crossed the street, anger at himself, at Lear Hendron, and mostly at the Ballards. Anger at himself for giving a damn one way or another as to how Lear Hendron felt toward him. Anger at the girl because of the empty, churned-up-inside feeling with which her distant, unassailable reserve always left him. Anger at the Ballards because they were the Ballards.

The hard brown planes of his face were pulled taut and the gray of his eyes took on a darker shade. "The Ballards," he muttered. "The damned, worthless, troublemaking Ballards, who good men have to coddle and nurse along because they were Abel Hendron's nephews, when a three-way hanging would be a blessing to the world. Yeah, the damned Ballards!"

The vehemence simmering in Kerchival made the swinging

doors of the Rialto winnow wide and violently as he shouldered through them. The first man he saw was Dusty Elliot, who let out a soft "Hah!" of relief. Ten feet beyond Dusty along the bar was Virg Hendron, spoiled, sarcastic, never letting anyone forget for a moment that he was heir apparent of the big War Hatchet outfit and the apple of his father's eye. Virg, half drunk, paid no attention to Kerchival's entrance, but was watching the group still farther down the bar, where the Ballards—Spence, Gard, and Turk—had formed a rough half circle about old Bill Yeager and were badgering and taunting him.

Kerchival dropped in beside Dusty Elliot and murmured: "No luck with Joe Orchard?"

"Joe's out of town," answered Dusty. "Man, am I glad to see you. This could get bad, Dave. They've been working on Yeager for the past hour, sinking the spurs a little deeper all the time. So far Bill's stood 'em off, but he's beginning to sweat. It's none of my pie, maybe, but right now I'm set to take a hand."

"My chore," said Kerchival. Then he added as a bleak afterthought: "By request."

He moved on down beside Virg Hendron. He nudged Virg with an elbow and said quietly: "Call 'em off, Virg."

Virg swung his head. Too much liquor had weakened his chin, and it wobbled slightly as anger flared in him. "Call 'em off? Why should I? They're doing all right with that damned old fool. He aims to sell us slope ranchers out to the plains outfits again this summer, just like he did last. Call 'em off nothing!"

"Call 'em off . . . or I will," warned Kerchival curtly.

"You'll mind your own business and leave well enough alone," said Virg thickly. "That's an order, Kerchival, with me, Virg Hendron, giving it."

Dave Kerchival looked this young fellow up and down in cool contempt. "Don't try and go proud on me, Virg," he said softly. "I can see right through you, because there ain't much there. So, if you won't, I will."

Kerchival turned away, took one stride, and stopped. There was a round, hard pressure against the small of his back and a slightly wild note in Virg Hendron's insistence.

"I'm telling you to mind your own business, Kerchival. And I won't tell you again."

Kerchival heard Dusty Elliot's soft curse of anger, and his first glance as he twisted his head was at Dusty, warning him off. Looking down over his shoulder, Kerchival saw that the hammer of Virg Hendron's gun was down and that Virg's thumb was not locked about it. So Kerchival whirled, grabbed, and twisted. With his free hand he caught the gun just before it dropped from Virg's half-paralyzed fingers. Still gripping Virg's agonized wrist, he gave a drive of added pressure, which wrung a yell of drunken pain from Virg and sent him staggering and floundering halfway to the door.

"Watch him, Dusty!" rapped Kerchival.

With Virg's gun balanced loosely in his hand, Kerchival turned back to the main issue. There was a hot, brittle anger seething all through him now. In the past he'd taken a lot from Virg Hendron, but so far had managed to keep his hands off him. This time, however, Virg had thrown a gun, and there were limits to that sort of thing, even from the son of Abel Hendron. Now for the Ballards, and, if they wanted something, they could damned well have it.

Intent on their rawhiding of Bill Yeager, the Ballards had paid no attention to Dave Kerchival's arrival in the saloon until Virg Hendron's yell of pain sounded. Now, startled and surlily uncertain, they came around to face Kerchival, who lashed them with a curt order.

"Break it up! Get out of here and leave Bill Yeager alone!"

They were three of a kind, these Ballards, three out of the same mold. There was a swarthiness in them, and their hair was coarsely black. They were thin and lank and narrow-featured, their eyes small and with a surface beadiness. There was, Dave Kerchival had always thought, a throwback to bad blood in them somewhere. Not from their mother's side, perhaps, for she, long dead now, had been Abel Hendron's only sister. And Kerchival had never heard Abel Hendron mention their father.

Whiskey brought out all the meanness in the Ballards, and Gard, the oldest of them, showed it now in the thin whip of his answer.

"You're ridin' the wrong horse, Kerchival. You may be foreman of War Hatchet, but that don't mean you can order us around."

"I'm telling you. Take your damned bully puss outside!"

Dusty Elliot said clearly: "I'm ridin' the same horse as Dave, ready for anything that shapes up. Steady does it."

Virg Hendron, rubbing his twisted arm, started to move back into this thing, circling a poker table to do so. Dusty met him before he could get around, grabbing him by the shoulder and slamming him into a chair.

"Stay there," warned Dusty. "Before you really get mussed up. You're gettin' out on a limb and it's crackin'." Virg cursed, but he stayed put.

Bill Yeager, the pressure off him, moved over beside Dave Kerchival. A man of medium size, the years had put a slight stoop to Yeager's shoulders, silvered his hair. He did not carry a gun, and his face, seamed and weathered, reflected a steady, quiet kindness that came from deep inside him. He said: "I would not have you in any trouble over me, Dave. They might have been pushing me a trifle heavy, but it's over now."

Kerchival, anger still crackling in him, said: "This is a pleasure, Bill, telling this crowd off. Something that's been long overdue." He looked past Yeager at the Ballards. "You heard me. Take your damned meanness outside!"

Kerchival had always figured that in a showdown Gard, as the oldest, would be the toughest of the Ballards, and he was watching him the closest. But it was Spence, the second of the brothers, who made the break. Spence was a morose, sullen sort, little given to talk, a thin curled lip token of the venom in him. Now, without the slightest warning, he went for his gun.

Kerchival had to reach clear past Gard to get at Spence. With Virg Hendron's gun naked and ready in his hand, Kerchival could have shot Spence dead in his tracks, but this thing had not gone that far yet and Kerchival had no wish that it should, so he slapped the barrel of the gun at the side of Spence's head, leaning forward, his arm at full reach. It was quite a stretch but he made it. Spence's eyes fluttered, his narrow, tight mouth sagged, and he went down.

Kerchival, carrying his lunge right on through, drove into Gard, knocking him back along the bar, pinning him there with an outflung left arm. The gun in Kerchival's right fist wove a deadly half circle, from Gard to Turk, then back to Gard again.

"I've had enough of this," he gritted harshly. "Anybody else makes a try for his gun, he really won't get there. Let this thing stand!"

At that moment the saloon doors winnowed and Abel Hendron came in, moving as he always did, spare, arrow-straight, with quick brisk steps. His voice held a cold and peremptory ring.

"What goes on in here?"

There was a moment of flat silence, then old Bill Yeager spoke, his voice slow and a little weary. "A little lesson in manners I guess you'd call it, Hendron. Dave, I'm mighty obliged to you."

Abel Hendron came along the bar, blinking his hard brown eyes to adjust them to the partial gloom of the saloon after the open white glare of the outside sunlight. He stopped, rising a trifle on his toes as he looked down at Spence Ballard.

"Gun-whipped?" he demanded bleakly.

"That's right," answered Kerchival. "I did it. He was drawing on me." Kerchival tossed Virg Hendron's gun up and down on an open hand. "I took this off Virg. He had it jammed up against my spine. I don't take that from any man, including Virg."

"I don't like this at all, Mister Kerchival," stated Abel Hendron, his voice very tight. "No, I don't like it at all."

Kerchival shrugged. "Neither do I. But the Ballards and Virg were full of red-eye and pushing Bill Yeager around. You notice Bill hasn't a gun, which is his usual way. It was something I couldn't stand for and it needed breaking up. So. . . ."

There were depths to this man Abel Hendron that Dave Kerchival had never been able to probe, but he knew him well enough to see that behind Hendron's hard brown eyes and thin-pressured lips a furious anger was raging. Anger perhaps at his son Virg for being the weak sister he was, and at the Ballards for being unable to carry through what they had started. But most of that anger would be directed at him, and this could well mean his job. But Kerchival met and held Hendron's boring glance without excuse or apology.

Abel Hendron swung his head toward the bartender. "How did you see it, Ney?"

Ed Ney spread both hands on the bar top and gave Hendron as good as he sent.

"Exactly like Dave said. I heard him ask Virg to call the Ballards off Yeager, and Virg wouldn't do it. He told Dave to keep out of it. When Dave turned his back and started to move in, Virg shoved a gun against his spine. Dave took it away from him and told the Ballards to back away. Spence went for his gun, and Dave clipped him. Dave could have shot Spence in half, and, had I been in his boots, I'd have done it. That's how it happened."

Hendron turned to Gard Ballard, his voice like the lash of a whip. "You and Turk get Spence out of here and take him home. Stay there until I say different. Virg, you go over to the Starlight and wait there for me."

It was plain that Gard would have liked to argue, but Turk, the youngest, said: "Shut up and gimme a hand with Spence. We're doin' no good here now."

Between them they got the half-stunned Spence to his feet and steered his shambling steps out into the street. Kerchival, who had been punching the shells out of the weapon, sent Virg's gun skidding across the top of the poker table. "Yours, Virg."

Virg took the weapon sulkily, holstered it, and followed the Ballards out.

Abel Hendron turned to Bill Yeager. "My apologies for their actions, Mister Yeager. I hope this won't affect the talk I want to have with you?"

"I doubt we need a talk," Yeager said in his quiet, slow way. "I know what you are going to ask of me, and I must say no. I will not now, or at any other time, close that herd trail up Kingfisher. Brace Shotwell, Joe Kirby, and the other plains outfits have as much right to the summer range on top of Mount Cherokee plateau as you or I or any other man. I have already seen Shotwell and Kirby and have told them they can take their herds through this summer the same as in years past."

Abel Hendron rocked back and forth from heel to toe, his eyes boring brown sparks. "That is your last word?"

"My last word," answered Bill Yeager. "I'm sorry we don't see things alike, Hendron. But I want to be friendly with all my neighbors."

Hendron turned his back on Bill Yeager. Curtly he said: "We'll be getting along now, Mister Kerchival. And you, Elliot."

He went out, erect, crisp-striding as he had come in. Dusty Elliot said *sotto voce:* "The King has spoken. Long live the King."

16

Bill Yeager stuck out a gnarled palm to Dave Kerchival. "Thanks again, son. Hope you won't hold it against me for not seeing eye to eye with your boss?"

Kerchival smiled grimly as he gripped the old cattleman's hand. "Every man has a right to his own opinion, Bill. Yours is a good one. Hang onto it."

As Kerchival and Dusty went out into the street, Kerchival dropped a hand on his companion's shoulder. "Better watch yourself, cowboy. You go making public cracks against your boss, you're liable to find yourself out of a job."

"Hah!" exclaimed Dusty. "I should worry about my job. You're the little cookie who better start worrying. You laid rough hands on the heir to greatness and put a dent in the hard skull of one of the precious nephews. Yeah, you better do the worrying. But honest, Dave, there's times when Abel Hendron's strut damn' near turns me inside out. What manner of man is he, anyhow? I been a War Hatchet hand for quite some time now and I still don't know that man."

"You know him as well as I do," said Kerchival. "Thanks for siding me in there."

Dusty snorted in high temper. "Now just who in hell would I side if it wasn't you? Not Virg or the Ballards, that's for sure."

There came a sharp clip-clopping of hoofs and Deputy Sheriff Joe Orchard rode into town through the alley between Sam Liederman's store and Ling Foy's A-1 Hash House. As he rode across the street, the deputy cocked an observing head over his shoulder, then dismounted and tied at the rail before his own office, with its jail out back. He was watching Gard and Turk Ballard trying to get Spence into his saddle. Spence was arguing, his voice, thin, hard, and profane, running along the street. Joe Orchard went over to them.

Virg Hendron was just disappearing into the Starlight, and Abel Hendron was stamping up the steps. Gil Lambie was letting his tired stage team walk the two hundred yards along to Bus Spurgeon's livery barn and corrals. On the bench near the door of Liederman's store, Jack Tully sucked at his cold pipe, apparently engrossed in nothing but his own thoughts. But far back in his pouchy, lidded eyes a sardonic light was gleaming, as though he found the world, and the men who moved through it, mockingly amusing.

Dusty Elliot said: "I'm still wonderin' where we go when we leave War Hatchet, Dave."

"You're worse than an old woman when it comes to worrying," accused Kerchival. "Never borrow trouble, cowboy. If it's headed your way, it will arrive, all in good time and of its own accord."

"I ain't worryin'," denied Dusty. "I'm just wonderin'."

"And over nothing, as far as we know now," Kerchival supplied.

"Uhn-uh," grunted Dusty. "Not over nothing. You and me . . . *you* in particular . . . just done things that ain't done by a War Hatchet hired hand, not and stay hired. If you think Abel Hendron is goin' to love you more after today, why, then you're crazy as a chickadee."

Kerchival paused at the lower step of the hotel, shrugged. "We'll see."

He laid a brief glance along the street. Spence Ballard was in his saddle now, and Joe Orchard had a shoulder point hitched indolently against the front of his office. He stayed that way until the Ballards, with Spence hunched low in his saddle, rode out of town. Then he turned in at his office door. Kerchival climbed the steps and went into the hotel.

Abel Hendron was waiting for him in the foyer. Virg wasn't in sight, but Lear Hendron stood over by one of the front windows, apparently engrossed in something outside. But her face was pale and troubled, and Kerchival doubted if she was really interested in anything the street held.

When Abel Hendron spoke, Dave Kerchival was slightly surprised, for Hendron's words had to do, not with the recent past unpleasantness that had taken place in the Rialto, but with the business that had taken Kerchival down into the horse ranch country beyond Fort Devlin.

"Did you have any success about those replacements for our cavvy herd, Mister Kerchival?"

It was Abel Hendron's way, this formality of address, even with his foreman. It was a part of the man's austere, inflexible make-up, something that had come down all the way through the years with him since the days when he had ridden as a young officer of cavalry in the Indian wars.

"I got what you sent me after." Kerchival nodded. "Thirty head. Fifteen from Leacock and fifteen from Brownson. Nothing younger than three years, nothing older than five. I put each one under saddle and tried it out thoroughly before I accepted it. Every animal sound as a nut. You'll get your money's worth in those horses. Both Brownson and Leacock promised delivery within the next two weeks."

Abel Hendron's hair, eyebrows, mustache, and neatly trimmed goatee were iron gray. His face was small-boned, and his skin, though tanned, was as fine-textured as that of a woman. Hard, unyielding pride lay in the man like a taut current. While Dave Kerchival was speaking, Hendron's eyes, so brown and queerly hard, stared flintily. And Kerchival, meeting the look steadily, wondered what the thoughts were that lay behind it. Kerchival had worked for Hendron for five years, but he had never been able to get past the man's hard armor and glimpse fully what lay in the frosty mind beyond.

Hendron said: "Very good, Mister Kerchival. A pity that the same allegiance to War Hatchet interests could not have guided you equally well in that affair in the Rialto."

Kerchival's eyes went cool and took on a hardness of their own. "I don't see where allegiance to War Hatchet had anything to do with that. A fine old gentleman was being pushed around, and I just couldn't go for that."

"It was none of your affair," insisted Abel Hendron. "Why did you make it so?"

Kerchival shrugged, said nothing, knowing it would do no good. It was useless to argue against the set mind of Abel Hendron. Either you conceded the argument to Hendron, or you let it hang in mid-air and die there. He would let this one die that way, Kerchival decided. Then, in the next moment, a queer, singing warmth ran through him, for, over by the window, Lear Hendron turned and spoke.

"He made it so, at least in part, because I asked him to, Father. He didn't know anything was going on in the Rialto until I told him. He had just arrived on the stage. What he did was largely at my request."

Abel Hendron half turned, started to say something, then locked compressed lips over the words and held them back. The muscles of his face tightened until his features seemed to draw almost to a point. If anger seethed in the man, and it seemed to, then he held it back until he was fully master of himself again. When he finally spoke, his words were as thin and dry as ashes.

"We will speak about this later . . . all of us. For the present, our business here in town is finished. Lear, I will expect you home by the time I arrive. That is all, Mister Kerchival."

Lear Hendron moved past her father and Kerchival with her head high, her eyes straight ahead. From the porch of the hotel she called: "Get the buckboard, Dusty!"

Kerchival went out. He had a horse at Bus Spurgeon's livery barn. He caught up his gripsack from where he'd first left it on

the hotel porch and called to Dusty, who had just started up the
street.

"Haul this home for me like a good feller. Catch!"

Dusty caught the tossed gripsack, went on his way. Kerchival
got out the makings, spun a cigarette into shape, supremely
conscious of this slim and silent girl who stood there on the
porch beside him. Without looking at her he spoke softly.

"That was a thoroughbred's move, Lear, speaking up for me.
But if it's going to bring you into an argument with your father,
I'm sorry you did it."

She shrugged wearily. "It doesn't matter. He was angry
anyhow and we all would have felt it, one way or another. Bill
Yeager . . . he wasn't hurt?"

"Not a finger laid on him."

"That at least is something." She was silent a moment, then
added: "Thank you."

"No need of that," murmured Kerchival. "I'm fond of Bill
Yeager myself. Not enough like him in this old world. Lear, I'm
trying to think how long it's been since I heard you laugh. And
how long it's been since you went to a dance, and how long
since I've danced with you. Too long, Lear. I'm wondering if
there is something I can do to help bring back the old days?
Better days than these have been of late."

He looked at her and saw faint color steal into her face. But
she shook her head and said: "There is nothing wrong with the
days. It is only the people who fill them."

With this surprising statement she went swiftly down the
steps and along the street, moving out to meet Dusty Elliot,
who was getting the buckboard away from the hitch rail in front
of Liederman's store. When Dusty pulled in beside her, she
found the step and was up and in, swiftly, lightly. Dusty swung
the rig in a skidding circle and boomed off along the street.

Moving slowly, Dave Kerchival, a big man who moved lightly

despite the weight of his puzzled thoughts, went up toward the livery barn. Now just what the devil, he mused, did Lear Hendron mean by her final words? Was the edge of them directed at him in person, or toward the world in general? Thinking back, he could not, for the life of him, recall anything he had done to set her too far up on her haughty ear. He concluded, a trifle moodily, that any man who tried to figure a woman's mind and moods might just as well try to see what lay behind the stars. He'd have just as much luck.

When, fifteen minutes later, he came back on the street leading his saddle horse, Dave Kerchival saw Abel Hendron heading for Sam Liederman's store, saw him pause and speak for a moment with Jack Tully, who still sat on the bench beside the door.

Kerchival swung into the saddle, turned his face to the fast upsweeping climb of the Mount Cherokee plateau, and lifted his horse into movement.

The street stood empty. The shadows beyond the buildings lay blacker and longer. Jack Tully stirred at last from his seat by Sam Liederman's door and ambled off along the street with the air of a man with nowhere to go and going there. Only his eyes seemed fully alert and they burned with that same queer light of inward mockery.

CHAPTER TWO

Dave Kerchival left the War Hatchet bunkhouse in the chilled dawn of a new day. He'd stayed up rather late the night before, expecting at any moment a call from Abel Hendron to report over to the big, sprawling ranch house. But none had come and this very silence had seemed an ill omen in Dusty Elliot's judgment.

"He's buildin' up his mad," Dusty had muttered for Kerchival's ears alone, when they finally turned in. "Tomorrow the big blow-up comes, sure as shootin'. You'll see, Dave."

Well, now it was tomorrow, and whatever came, Kerchival told himself, he wasn't going to worry about it, one way or another. He had no apologies to make for what he'd done in the Rialto the previous afternoon, and he wasn't going to make any. If that didn't suit Abel Hendron, well—the world was wide and there were a lot of trails a man could ride over. There might be just one regret. Lear Hendron. Though she had never given Dave Kerchival any particular reason to feel that she saw him in any other light than just another hired hand of her father's, it was Kerchival's thought that no man who had looked upon Lear Hendron and been anywhere near her could ride away and forget her with ease. True, once or twice in the old days there had been times when she had shown Kerchival a momentary softness, moments when a fresh, unspoiled girlishness had shone forth. But events of later days had convinced Kerchival that, if there was any particular sentiment, it lay wholly within him and not in her. And it might be just as well if he set about right now to rid himself of it.

Over at the cook shack a thin blue haze of wood smoke crept shiveringly from the stovepipe, scenting the air with pine resin, and signaling that Deaf Blair, the War Hatchet cook, was up and about his business. Kerchival went over there, poured icy water into the wash basin by the cook shack door, plunged into it, and came up blowing and scrubbing his face furiously.

The shock of the water drove any lingering drowsiness out of him, whipped the blood to his face, and set it to tingling. Engrossed in his sputtering ablutions, he did not hear a horse come plodding slowly up past the corrals, and it was not until he was working eagerly with a rough towel that he became aware of Deputy Sheriff Joe Orchard, his fleece-coated shoulders hunched against the early morning's cold, crossed forearms resting on his saddle horn. Joe Orchard's horse was panting from the long haul up the slope, and its breath smoked about its nostrils in the biting chill.

Kerchival grinned past the folds of his busily working towel. "Hi, Joe! Riding mighty early, ain't you? Don't tell me that somebody has busted the law."

Joe Orchard nodded, his leathery features gravely expressionless. "Somebody did. They dry-gulched Bill Yeager."

Kerchival lowered the towel, staring. "Joe . . . you can't mean that! Not old Bill Yeager . . . dry-gulched?"

"Bill's dead," said Joe Orchard. "He staggered into my office around eight o'clock last night, drilled through and through and dying on his feet. He'd come in afoot, and how he did it I don't know. Neither does Doc Cable. He lasted only about half an hour after that."

Kerchival began making little aimless dabs with the towel, half of them missing his face entirely. He seemed like a man dazed from a vicious and unexpected blow. Then his face became solid and set and grave and his eyes turned dark. His voice ran weightily with a vast and bitter anger and regret.

"God must hate a dirty, sneaking dry-gulcher. Bill Yeager was a damned fine man. And they did that to him? Poor old Bill. . . ." His voice ran off and broke in a brittle monotone.

He stared at nothing and his eyes pinched down at the corners. He shook himself and said: "Light down, Joe. You look like you could stand a shot of hot coffee."

Joe Orchard, a little old and tired and disillusioned, swung from his saddle. He'd seen his share of treachery and brutality and it had left him taciturn and brusquely armored. He looped the reins about the saddle horn, slapped an open palm against his horse's flank, and the animal trotted back to the corrals where it might nose at others of its kind across the zigzag of a stake-and-rider rail fence.

In the cook shack there was warmth and the savory promise of breakfast to come. Deaf Blair nodded to Joe Orchard and passed over a blackened coffee pot. Dave Kerchival poured two big cups and gave Joe Orchard one of them. The deputy cradled the cup between both hands as though to warm them. "I'm making a routine check," he said. "You came straight home, Dave, when you left town yesterday afternoon?"

"Straight home, Joe."

"How about Dusty?"

"He drove Lear home. He was unhooking the buckboard team when I rode in."

"And Abel Hendron?"

"He rode in about an hour after I did. Virg was with him."

"What about the rest of the outfit?"

"Perk O'Dair and Chick Roland came in a little later. They'd been combing the shale country up under the rim, looking for strays. But those two kids wouldn't hurt a fly."

Joe Orchard took a deep drag of coffee, smacked his lips.

"No," he agreed, "they wouldn't. Matter of fact, I know the same of you and Dusty, of course. I ain't looking at any of you officially. I'm just asking questions . . . sort of getting the lay of the checkerboard clear in my mind. But . . . how about the Ballards?"

Kerchival hunched his big shoulders. "Now you're whittling, Joe. But I wouldn't know a damned thing about them. Your guess is just as good as mine, there." He was still a moment, brooding, then added: "After the ruckus in the Rialto, Abel Hendron ordered them home and told them to stay there until he said different. They did leave town. I know that, but I don't know another damned thing."

"While you were in the Rialto, did you happen to hear any of them make an actual threat against Yeager?"

Kerchival shook his head. "No, can't say that I did. I know they were bullyragging him pretty heavy, whether just for damned ornery meanness or trying to get old Bill to make a pass at one of them and give them excuse to maul him, I couldn't say. But things kind of added up quick when I got in there, and what jawing took place then was pretty much between the Ballards and Virg Hendron and me. Maybe Ed Ney would know something about that."

Joe Orchard shook his head. "Talked to Ed last night. He gave me just about the same picture you do."

Deaf Blair slid a couple of plates of steak and potatoes across the table, and Kerchival and Joe Orchard fell to. Before they had finished, the rest of the War Hatchet crew came straggling in, sleepy, numbed from the outside chill. They nodded to Joe Orchard and dug into their breakfasts. His plate clean, Joe Orchard jerked a slight nod to Kerchival, who followed him outside and over to his horse. Orchard spun a cigarette into shape, lighted it, and flipped the still burning match into a clump of dew-drenched grass, where it sputtered and went out with a little, thin hiss.

"Mostly what I came out this way for, Dave, besides giving you the word about Bill Yeager, was to tell you that Mel Rhodes wants to see you. I told you how Bill Yeager came into my office. Before he died, he made a will. He wouldn't let me or Doc Cable try and plug up his wounds. He said it was too late to do any good, which was true enough, I reckon, with him knowing it. All Bill wanted was to see Mel Rhodes . . . quick!

"Well, I got hold of Mel, and for a little time Bill talked fast, with Mel Rhodes taking it all down on a piece of legal paper. This was Bill's will. Doc Cable had to give Bill a shot of something to hold him together long enough to sign that will. But he did it. Then he watched me and Mel and Doc witness it. Then he died. That will should interest you a lot, Dave. For in it he left everything he owned to you."

Kerchival was building a smoke. It took a second or two for the full significance of Joe Orchard's final words to take effect. Then Kerchival's head jerked up and he said harshly: "That's a hell of a lousy joke, Joe."

"No joke." Joe Orchard shrugged. "I read the will. I know."

The partly built cigarette in Kerchival's fingers tore in half and a little cascade of brown tobacco flakes spilled down. "But it doesn't make sense, Joe. It doesn't add up. Why . . . ?"

Joe Orchard shrugged again. "Whether it makes sense or not, that's the way it is. I don't know why, though maybe I got a hunch. Anyhow, range, cows, brand, headquarters, bank account . . . the whole chivaree . . . it all goes to you, Dave. Mel Rhodes has the will locked up in his safe. He wants to see you about it and I told him I'd tell you. Now I got work to do. A man's been murdered. A good man. Just about the best damn' man in this whole stretch of country. Before I'm done, I'll see somebody hung for that killing."

Joe Orchard wasn't bragging. He wasn't that sort. He wasn't

an impressive-looking man in an over-all glance. Years, and a habitual taciturnity, had given him a slightly faded look of neutrality. Until you came to his eyes. There, any observing man found reason for pause and careful stepping. Joe Orchard wasn't one to push his authority around, but once that authority was needed it was never found wanting.

He stepped into his saddle, settled himself. Dave Kerchival was reluctant to have him leave. He dropped a hand on Joe's knee.

"This floors me, Joe . . . it really does. I just can't figure why. . . . I'd known Bill Yeager for quite a time. I liked him and I think he liked me. But then, Bill was the sort to like anybody who met him halfway fair."

"You took some weight off his neck in the Rialto yesterday, didn't you?" reminded the deputy.

"I suppose I did. But what the hell! If I hadn't done it, then Dusty Elliot would have. And before he saw the Ballards get too rough with old Bill, I think Ed Ney would probably have bought in. A man doesn't will you a ranch just because you haul a bunch of drunks off his back."

"Bill Yeager was a mild man, a gentle one. Some people might even have called him a meek man," observed Joe Orchard. "And me, I've found that when all the chips are down, it can often be the meek man who is the toughest fighter. These wild, rip-roaring boys make a lot of fuss and noise, but mostly they ain't too hard to cut down to size. Because it's all physical with them. You get there first with a gun and the catamounts quit squalling for trouble and become kittens purring for peace. But the meek man, he fights with his head. He thinks. And when he gets through thinking, why, then you find yourself tied hard and fast. Bill Yeager was the sort never to lift his hand against any man, but when the tally is all written he still comes in the winner."

This was a long speech for Joe Orchard to make, but it

showed an insight and keen observation that left Dave Kerchival at once puzzled and understanding. He stared after Joe Orchard gravely as the deputy rode away.

Over east, past the distant shoulder of Mount Cherokee, the world was silver and rose where the sun was preparing a blazing pathway across the heavens that had begun to warm and glow. Dave Kerchival watched that building color and tried to get a full hold on this staggering fact that had been tossed into his lap.

Perk O'Dair and Dusty Elliot came out of the cook shack, rolling their after-breakfast smokes. Dusty asked: "What's Joe Orchard ridin' so early for, Dave?"

Kerchival's tone was somber. "I hate to spoil the makings of a fine day for you, boys. But somebody dry-gulched Bill Yeager."

"No!" Dusty came up as though kicked in the belly. "You don't mean that, fellah! Not Bill Yeager?"

Kerchival nodded grimly. "It's so, Dusty."

Dusty Elliot had a round and ruddy face, with the most cheerful blue eyes in the world, a gay and optimistic sort, who could see sunshine in the midst of a winter blizzard. That was Dusty. But now all the cheer faded and his face twisted in misery.

"That's bad. That's rotten! Bill was such a good old *hombre*. What breed of damned snake . . . when . . . where . . . ?"

"Late yesterday afternoon or early yesterday evening, I guess," said Kerchival. "I don't know just where. Joe didn't know that, either. Bill managed to get back to town, to Joe Orchard's office, but he was dying when he got there."

"Then maybe he had some idea who did it? He could have told Joe."

Kerchival shook his head. "Joe would have known where to look if Bill had told him. But Bill didn't know."

29

Dusty and Perk had been full of warm breakfast and ready to meet a cheerful day on the basis of it. But this dire news turned them stony. Perk, still a kid barely into his twenties, spoke woodenly.

"I'd sure enjoy pullin' on the rope that swung the guy who did that dirty trick. More'n once I've stopped by Bill Yeager's Lazy Y headquarters. He was allus friendly, allus ready to brew a pot of java, and spare an hour to swap the breeze. Dammit, I feel sick!"

Perk turned away, kicking a scuffed boot toe against the dewy earth.

Over at the main ranch house a screen door slammed. It was Virg Hendron coming out, and he headed straight for them. There was a smug look mixed with the sulkiness about his mouth and a taunting triumph in his eyes. He spoke curtly.

"The old man wants to see you, Kerchival. O'Dair, catch up and saddle that claybank gelding of mine."

Virg Hendron moved on toward the cook shack, swaggering a little. Perk stared after him, mumbling: "I like my job and all that, but one of these days I'm gonna treat myself to one supreme pleasure. I'm gonna back that jigger up against a corral fence and just naturally whip the everlasting hell right out of him." Perk swung his shoulders restlessly, then added in rough mimicry: "O'Dair, catch up and saddle my bronc'! Just like he was talkin' to a mongrel dog."

"Keep your shirt on, kid," counseled Kerchival. "This won't be the first bronco you've saddled."

Perk headed for the corrals, scuffing his spurs. "Got a notion to put a bur under the saddle blanket, and then watch Mister Virg Hendron get tossed plumb to hell-and-gone."

Dusty Elliot spoke softly: "So Abel Hendron wants to see you, and this early in the morning. Sounds like he'd made up his mind on somethin'. This may be it, Dave."

"May be, Dusty," conceded Kerchival. "But he doesn't want to start laying on the rawhide too heavy. I'm in no mood right now to take anything from anybody. And it could be that I got news of my own that will jar him . . . plenty."

"Remember . . . if he ties the boot to you, he can make it double," vowed Dusty. "I'll be taggin' along."

"That's what you think!" said Kerchival across his shoulder. "I'll have something to say about that."

Abel Hendron and his daughter Lear were just sitting down to breakfast when Kerchival strode in, hat in hand. By the white, silent look of the girl, Kerchival knew that a storm of some kind had been taking place in this ranch house. There was a fixed thinness to Abel Hendron's lips, and it was Dave Kerchival's thought that, if this summons was for the purpose of firing him, then it was as deeply indicative of Abel Hendron's make-up as anything could be. It meant that Hendron couldn't wait an extra moment before hitting at someone who had, in his eyes, offended his sense of authority and possession.

Kerchival said: "You wanted to see me."

"Yes." Abel Hendron's answering word was as concise and definite as the cut of a knife. "For five years you have worked for me, Mister Kerchival. For the past two of those years you have been my foreman. You have been a good foreman and for that reason I have overlooked certain incidents in the past when you chose to argue certain points of ranch policy with me. But yesterday you stepped completely out of bounds. For one thing, you took the part of a man who has consistently refused to co-operate with me in matters concerning the Mount Cherokee plateau range that would have been of mutual benefit to both him and myself. In addition to that, you laid violent hands on my son and you used a gun barrel on one of my nephews. There can be no forgiveness for that, Mister Kerchival."

Frost and smoke began gathering in Dave Kerchival's eyes.

For a long time he had stood for this stiff, precise man's arrogant pride and unbending formality, viewing it with a sort of tolerant humor, seeing in it the form of Hendron's military training that had left him the complete martinet, where it would not have affected a broader man at all. In the past Kerchival had never bothered to analyze Hendron's manner particularly, but now, standing here meeting those hard brown eyes with a brand-new scrutiny, he saw things he'd never seen before.

He saw selfishness, he saw smallness, he saw certain weaknesses that Hendron's armor of formality was calculated to hide and cover up. He saw the hint of things worse than that. Cruelty, for one. So now Kerchival laughed abruptly, not with humor, but, instead, with a vast scathing.

The tone of that laugh brought Abel Hendron jerking up, stiff and startled, in his chair. His hands, spread palms down on the table top a moment before, now clenched into fists.

"You'd laugh at me?" demanded Hendron

"Yeah," drawled Kerchival, "I laugh at you. I laugh at your insufferable pomp and strut and blind conceit. I laugh at your pose of righteousness with which you try and cover up some things you'd rather the world wouldn't see. As for that spoiled, slickery pup you claim as a son, he pulled a gun on me. I've taken plenty from him in the past, but I don't take that from him or any other man. I did you a favor in merely taking the gun away from him instead of jamming it down his drunken throat, like he deserved. Your precious nephew, Spence Ballard, threw a gun on me with open intention. I could have shot his head off and had clear self-defense, as Ed Ney so informed you. But again I did you a favor. I merely buffaloed him.

"Now what do you do? Do you go after Virg and Spence Ballard and give them what for, which they both deserve? No. You cover up their worthless hides and instead try and read me off as though you were high lord of all creation and I some kind of sniveling, cowering worm. Which is your mistake. Is it any wonder that I laugh?"

Never before had Abel Hendron been spoken to in this way by a hired hand. Never before, for that matter, had any man torn past the chinks of his formal armor and flayed him in the raw. So now a hectic flush gathered under his eyes, congesting them. His lips pulled to a thin and bloodless line. For a moment he was stiff and speechless with rage.

Lear Hendron, a still and white-faced witness to it all, got abruptly to her feet and ran out of the room. At this Dave Kerchival's eyes softened slightly in a brief regret. Then they filled with smoke and frost again.

Abel Hendron finally got words past his stiff lips, and, while they were as formal and clearly enunciated as ever, they now held an ugly turgidity.

"Mister Kerchival, you are discharged. You will leave this ranch within the hour. You will never put foot on my range again. You will not speak to my daughter. You will leave me and mine completely alone. You will, in fact, be very wise if you get completely out of this part of the country. Is that understood?"

Kerchival built a steady-fingered cigarette, studying musingly this man across the table from him, and his thought was that Abel Hendron was little short of preposterous. Could the man really believe that his dictatorial tirade and manner could have any lasting effect on another who was completely free and his own man?

The by-play of words and wills and anger of the past minute or two again showed Kerchival what he had been blind to before. Yes, for the first time he had really broken past the inflexible mask to Abel Hendron's mind, past those hard brown eyes to what lay behind them. What he saw definitely wasn't pretty. It was ugly, full of shadows. And full of what now would be a never-ending, unrelenting hate. Kerchival spoke evenly. "It's just as well that I am leaving. Your firing me may give you some satisfaction, but it really doesn't mean a thing. For I would have left anyhow. There is something you don't know, Hendron. Joe Orchard was through very early this morning. He brought some sad news. Bill Yeager is dead. He was dry-gulched."

Kerchival watched Abel Hendron closely as he spoke, alert to Hendron's reactions to this word. He saw Hendron go very still. Then be shrugged. "I'm not hypocrite enough to say I will mourn greatly. The man had been in my way for a long time. Perhaps by that statement you may incline to the belief that I had a hand in Yeager's death?" Here was a thread of mockery.

"Not necessarily," retorted Kerchival bluntly. "Yet I've come to the point where I wouldn't put such a thing past you. You see, Hendron, for the first time I've come to the point where I believe I really know you. No, I wouldn't put that sort of thing past you, nor a lot of other things. Of one thing I'm sure. The whelp who dry-gulched Bill Yeager will either hang or end up strung on a Forty-Five slug. Some of us who knew Bill Yeager for his real worth are going to make it our personal chore to see to that. But I've still further news for you, and there'll be no satisfaction in this for you at all."

"If it is some kind of empty threat," said Hendron, shrugging again, "I'm not concerned with hearing it. It will mean nothing to me. You'd better leave, Mister Kerchival."

"With pleasure . . . presently," shot back Kerchival coldly. "What I was going to say is this. Bill Yeager did not die at the spot where he was dry-gulched. He managed to get into town, to Joe Orchard's office. There he lived long enough to draw up a will, before reputable witnesses. In that will Bill Yeager left his ranch and everything he owned to me. Does that register, Hendron?"

He did not need Hendron's answer to see that it did, very definitely. Abel Hendron came fully to his feet, leaning across the table. "You're lying!" he charged harshly. "You're lying in your teeth, Kerchival!"

Kerchival laughed mirthlessly again. "You know I'm not. You'd just like to believe that I am. Now I'm going to get my gear together. I'll be by for my time in about half an hour. Strange, isn't it, Hendron, how a man's trouble can breed and grow?"

Kerchival turned his back and walked out.

For a long, long minute Abel Hendron never moved; he just stared at the doorway through which Dave Kerchival had passed. Then he began pounding his hands against the table top in short, stiff, violent jabs. His thin drawn lips began to twist and writhe, and across them spilled a man's convulsed fury, in curses that were the more venomous because they were soundless. For this moment, with no one to see, Abel Hendron stripped the mask fully aside.

Dave Kerchival rode away from War Hatchet without hurry. In his five years with the outfit he'd accumulated more junk and gear than he had realized. Had he been going on the drift, looking for another job somewhere, he would have thrown a lot of the stuff away. But with a headquarters of his own to go to now, a place not too many miles away, he took most of the stuff along, feeling more or less like a country peddler with it all tied to his saddle.

Dusty Elliot had helped him get it together, and Kerchival had his hands full persuading Dusty to stay on at War Hatchet, at least for a time, though Dusty was all foamed up about asking for his own time.

"You stick on here, Dusty," Kerchival had told him, "until I get a few angles straightened out. Once I see where I can use you, I'll let you know. Then you can come a-running."

Grumpily Dusty had finally agreed to this arrangement.

"But," he had declared, "from here on out I ain't takin' a thing from Abel Hendron and even less than that from the precious son. Virg so much as looks cross-eyed at me, I'll hit him so hard he'll stay that way. There's just one person on this ranch now who can give me a call down, and she won't. Dave, I'm damn' sorry for Lear Hendron. She's not like the rest of 'em. That girl is the pure quill. Havin' to put up with a father an' a brother like she's got must be hell, pure and simple."

To which Kerchival had nodded. "I agree with you there, Dusty," he had said soberly.

When, ready to leave, Kerchival had gone up to get his time, he had found Abel Hendron sitting, stiff and pokerfaced, at his old desk in the small corner room of the ranch house that he used as an office. Hendron was master of himself again, though there were little white cavities at the corners of his arched, patrician nostrils. But a nagging question was eating at him and he had to voice it as he had handed over Kerchival's final pay check.

"You tell me you are now the owner of the Lazy Y. What is going to be your attitude toward the plains herds, Mister Kerchival? Will they still be allowed to use the Kingfisher Creek drive way up to the plateau for summer graze?"

Kerchival had answered with a single curt word. "Probably."

Abel Hendron had tapped stiff fingers on his desk top. "That would be a very foolish concession to make on your part, Mister Kerchival. Very foolish."

To this Kerchival had answered with a cold, contemptuous stare. "I won't be as easy to dry-gulch as Bill Yeager was. You see, Hendron, I am not so trustful of human nature and my fellow man as good old Bill. Any trouble pushed my way will be thrown back in the lap of him who starts it . . . and hard! That answer you?"

Kerchival had turned and left abruptly, despising this cold, precise man with the hard brown eyes, the blind, arrogant, hypocritical pride, and the masked, bleakly calculating mind.

From War Hatchet, Dave Kerchival let his horse drift downslope and to the west. In time he crossed Kingfisher Creek, climbed Butcherknife Ridge, and struck a trail that led to Lazy Y headquarters. Bill Yeager could have been a lot bigger cattleman than he was, for he had owned extensive range that could have grazed twice the number of cattle that carried his brand.

But Bill Yeager had been one of those fortunate men able to reduce the problem of living to its simplest formula. A man, so Yeager had reasoned, could eat only so much food, wear only so many clothes at a time, and sleep in only one bunk. These were the fundamental needs of life, and to try to enlarge on them was sheerest folly in his eyes.

So he had made no attempt to grow big for no purpose other than being big. He had run his spread without help, found a solitary satisfaction in living life as he liked it best, which was with a minimum of complications and without the conflicts bound to be inherent in the process of trying to push his way to larger size. A simple man with simple needs and the simple philosophy of live and let live. That had been Bill Yeager.

But, mused Dave Kerchival as he rode, thinking on these things, they wouldn't let old Bill live. They had shot him down from ambush, in the most cowardly of all killing ways. And who were they? The Ballards, maybe. Or Abel Hendron. Not by his own hand, of course. But by his plan and order, perhaps.

It wasn't a good thought. For in some vague way it touched at Lear Hendron, laid a smudge upon her. And that was a tough thought for Dave Kerchival to swallow.

It was Kerchival's intention to get rid of his load of gear at Lazy Y headquarters, see that any chance cattle or horses in the corrals were not suffering for lack of feed or water, and then head on to Warm Creek to see Mel Rhodes about that will.

Lazy Y headquarters lay on a spacious bench land under the still and lofty majesty of a stand of pillared sugar-pine timber. Kerchival had expected to find the place deserted and, therefore, he stood high in his saddle in surprise when he saw a full half-dozen saddle horses loafing around, reined about the cabin. On top of that a rider with a rifle in his hands stepped from the cabin door and dropped the weapon into line.

"Far enough for the moment, friend," he announced curtly. "You can stop right there!"

CHAPTER THREE

Dave Kerchival reined in, his glance roving, hardness building up in his eyes. He did not recognize this rider behind the threatening rifle, but he did know the raw-boned man who now stepped from the cabin and stopped beside the alert rifle holder. It was Brace Shotwell, one of the plains cattlemen. Kerchival eased back in his saddle.

"What's this all about, Shotwell?"

As he spoke, Kerchival rode forward again, and the rifle lifted in line with his chest. But Brace Shotwell reached out and pushed the weapon aside, growling in deep, booming tones: "It's all right, Buck. I know this man." Of Kerchival, Shotwell asked: "Alone?"

"Alone." Kerchival nodded. "What brings you here?"

"Haven't you heard about Bill Yeager?"

"I heard. That's why I'm here."

"That's why we're here, too," Shotwell said. "I got the word late last night, so I figured to move in and make damn' sure nobody beat me to it. Come up early this morning."

"Which means," said Kerchival, "that you'll be starting your herds up to the plateau summer range before long and you wanted to make sure the trail was kept open. That it?"

"That's it. What did Hendron send you over here for? To take possession so he could block the trail, mebbe? By the look of the gear tied to your saddle you're intending on quite a stay."

Kerchival shook a slow head. "I came over to take possession all right, but not at Hendron's order. I'm all done with War Hatchet. Got paid off this morning."

Brace Shotwell was a man with the hard sun of the plains burned deeply in him and the tenacity that the tough plains built in a man who could set his roots in them and make them stick. He was a man not easily fooled, and now he eyed Kerchival narrowly.

"That listens good," said Shotwell skeptically, "but it might be a slick move by Hendron. For if you ain't figgering on taking over for Hendron, who are you taking over for?"

"Taking over for myself," Kerchival told him calmly. "Because it's mine. The whole Lazy Y layout. Before he died, Bill Yeager made a will and left everything to me."

"That," said Shotwell bluntly, "I got to see. Just don't make sense to me."

"Me, either," said the rider with the rifle. "This jigger a War Hatchet hand, Brace?"

"Last time I saw him he was," said Shotwell. "Name's Dave Kerchival. The War Hatchet *segundo.*"

By now there were other riders pushing out of the cabin. Kerchival caught a whiff of cooking coffee. Arriving early, these men were now putting together some breakfast.

Dave Kerchival hung onto his temper. He understood the position of these men. That herd trail between Kingfisher Creek and Butcherknife Ridge, over which in years past they had moved their herds up to the summer range on the plateau, was vitally important to them. For once the trail was closed they would be desperately up against it for grass to carry their herds through the long hot summer months down on the plains. While Bill Yeager had lived, the freedom of the herd trail was guaranteed. Now that he was dead, these men were only making certain that no one else moved in and closed it.

"Looks like there is only one way to convince you, Brace,"

said Kerchival quietly. "Suppose you leave your men here to hold onto things while you ride down to town with me and see Mel Rhodes. You'll be able to read the will yourself. I tell you I'm giving it to you straight. I'm all through with War Hatchet."

Again Shotwell searched Kerchival's face with narrowed eyes. He nodded grudgingly. "That listens fair," he admitted. "I'll do it." He turned to his men. "You boys stay put. Don't let anybody in here while I'm gone, no matter what kind of argument they put up." He went over and caught up the reins of one of the waiting horses.

Kerchival swung down. "I'm getting rid of all this gear. I'll leave it here. You see, I expect to be back."

Hard, suspicious eyes watched him as he unslung his stuff and stacked it against a corner of the cabin. These men were taking nothing for granted. Kerchival went back into his saddle and said: "All right, Brace."

They rode away, dropping off the shoulder of the bench, putting their horses to a jog down the winding trail. Below them through the miles the great slope fell away into a world still partly shrouded by morning mists that fought the burn of the early sun stubbornly. The great stretch of distant plains country was a vast, reaching gulf, a hard, tough country that bred hard, tough men.

It was Shotwell who finally broke the silence. "How did you come to know about Bill Yeager and hear of this will business, Kerchival?"

"Joe Orchard," Kerchival answered briefly. "Joe rode in to War Hatchet headquarters at break of day this morning. I admit I found it as hard to believe, at first, as you find it now. I mean about the will. But Joe insisted it was true, and he's not the sort to cook up fairy tales."

"No," conceded Shotwell, "he ain't."

Again they rode the miles down, and again silence held until, swinging with the massive curve of the plateau's flank, they came in sight of Warm Creek. Then it was Shotwell who spoke again.

"It's a big country and it can swallow lots of men without leaving a ripple. But there's some who leave a gap against the skyline when they're gone. Bill Yeager was such. He didn't strut, he didn't pose, he didn't make a big noise. But in his way he stood as tall as any man I've ever known. I'm not saying that just because he shot square with us fellers off the plains. It's something else. I reckon that behind the hard work and sweat most of us put out is the hope that we'll find some of the answers on how to wring the finest flavors out of living. Bill Yeager was one man to whom those answers came easy. Bill got a lot outta the earth and sky and the good things of life that don't cost any man a damn' cent. He was quite a man, and me, I'd deem it a high favor of the Lord was I to get the chance to look across the sights of a gun at the man who killed him. Yes, sir, that I would."

Kerchival, startled at such words from this leathery, horny-handed man of the plains, flashed a glance at him. "You put it mighty well, Brace. And you're right, all the way."

Shotwell got out a stubby pipe, began packing it. "None of my business, of course, but from what you said a while back you were set to cut the string at War Hatchet even if you'd never heard of a will. Something must have happened between you and Abel Hendron."

"Something did," said Kerchival laconically. "You know how those things are. This and that build up to a point and then bust."

"Strange man, Abel Hendron," observed Shotwell, entirely without rancor. "I could be around him for fifty years and still not know him."

"You, and others," agreed Kerchival dryly.

The town of Warm Creek was greeting another day with yawning leisure. Its windows flashed ruddily in the sunlight and its chimneys gave off lazy coils of smoke. Mel Rhodes's office was in the second story of Sam Liederman's store building, and Kerchival and Brace Shotwell reined in there. Buster, Sam's old dog, came, tail wagging, across the store porch, and Kerchival paused to give the old fellow a pat. Jack Tully was already holding down his usual place on the bench beside the door and he ducked his round head in greeting.

"Gentlemen! Another fine morning."

Climbing the stairway to Mel Rhodes's law office, Brace Shotwell said: "Now there's a strange one. Jack Tully, I mean. I can't remember ever hitting town but what I see him sitting on that bench, watching the world go by. Never heard of him doing a lick of work. Yet he gets by, fat and sassy. Some people sure got the problems of living figgered down to a science."

Kerchival chuckled. "I've heard Mel Rhodes say that Jack Tully was this town's unwelcome conscience. If a two-drink man takes three, Tully knows about it."

Mel Rhodes had his feet cocked on his desk and he was slouched so far down in his chair he seemed to be sitting on his shoulder blades. He was long and raw-boned and loose-jointed, with a shrewd, big-featured face and an unruly shock of brown hair. His office door was open, so Kerchival and Shotwell went right in.

"Been expecting you, Dave," Rhodes said. Then, a little pointedly: "Something you wanted to see me about, Shotwell?"

The plains cattleman shrugged. "Kerchival promised to show me something. A will."

"So-o?" Rhodes cocked a questioning eye at Kerchival, who explained the set-up at the Lazy Y headquarters.

"I didn't have too much luck convincing Brace, here, of my claim, so I invited him along to see for himself. I'm not blaming

43

him any for being a little skeptical, because I've had trouble convincing myself that the word Joe Orchard gave me about Bill Yeager's will is straight."

"Joe gave it to you straight, all right," said Mel Rhodes. He seemed almost to squirm out of his chair, one joint at a time. He went over to a small iron safe in the far corner of the office and returned with a folded paper. "Want to read it yourself, Shotwell, or will it satisfy you to listen while I read?"

"Hell, you read it, Mel," grunted Brace Shotwell. "Get me right. I'm not out to make trouble or start an argument. It's just that things have happened that I'm plenty concerned about, and I'm hoping certain matters won't change, even though Bill Yeager is gone. Yeah, you read it."

Mel Rhodes did. When he had finished, Shotwell nodded. "That's it, I reckon. It's just like you said, Dave. Well, I'll go back and call my boys off. It's your range, your headquarters."

Shotwell turned to leave, then paused as Dave Kerchival spoke.

"One minute, Brace. This thing is as new and startling to me as it is to you or anyone else. But it seems to be the real thing. Bill Yeager left me a ranch. I figure he left me something else, something that isn't written down. Call it an unspoken obligation, or a way of thinking and living, so that everybody gets a square shake. You'll be heading back to the plains. Take this word with you for yourself and Joe Kirby and the rest of the plains outfits who've been using that drive trail up Kingfisher to the plateau summer range. It will stay open, Brace . . . just like it was when Bill Yeager was alive."

Shotwell, partially turned, came all the way around, a gleam of relieved eagerness breaking up the hard gravity of his craggy face. "You mean that?"

Kerchival nodded. "Sure I mean it. What was good enough for Bill Yeager is good enough for me."

Shotwell stuck out his hand. "That's square, Dave . . . square as hell. That'll make good news for a lot of people."

As Brace Shotwell's spurs scuffed and clanked a fading way downstairs, Mel Rhodes murmured: "And bad news for certain others I might mention." He tossed the will over to Kerchival and said: "See with your own eyes."

Kerchival read slowly, thoroughly. These were Bill Yeager's dying words, but Mel Rhodes, in putting them down, had smoothed and sorted them, touched them with legal phraseology. But that scrawling, angular signature at the end—no one could touch or change that. That was all Bill Yeager's. His last living act. *William A. Yeager.* That was how he had written it, that was how it was. And then, as witnesses, the signatures of Mel Rhodes and Doc Cable and Joe Orchard.

"It's legal, Mel?" asked Dave Kerchival. "It would stand up in court?"

"Until Judgment Day," vowed Rhodes.

Kerchival scrubbed a hand across his face. "I've been trying to figure out why he picked me. I knew him pretty well . . . better than most, maybe. Still, I can't figure it. Wouldn't Bill have kin somewhere?"

Mel Rhodes shook his shaggy head. "No kin, Dave. I asked Bill about that. About the other angles, I've been doing a heap of thinking myself. I've come up with two answers. One you've already proven me right on, and proved Bill Yeager's judgment right, too. Which is that you're not shutting the plains herds out of the plateau range. Somewhere, sometime, you must have given Bill the feeling that you approved of his stand in that matter. Second reason . . . and I admit I'm throwing a long guess here . . . is that you know the mind and make-up of Abel Hendron as well as anyone and better than most."

Kerchival's eyes narrowed slightly. "What's that got to do with it?"

Mel Rhodes shrugged. "Do you know of anybody, outside of maybe the Ballards, more anxious to see that drive trail up Kingfisher Creek closed to the plains herds?"

"No," admitted Kerchival slowly, "I don't."

"Well," went on Rhodes, "I see that in Abel Hendron's head, and I see schemes reaching even farther . . . much farther. For that man, Dave, is cursed by more than just ego and a damned-fool suffocating thing that he calls pride. He wants the world, or a damned big chunk of it. Look here!" The lawyer caught up a pencil and paper and began sketching a rude map.

"Here's the Mount Cherokee plateau rim. Here are the plains. In between is all of the slope range. Kingfisher Creek comes down all the way from the rim . . . so. Maybe five miles west of Kingfisher, Warm Creek comes down. All of the slope east of Kingfisher is controlled by War Hatchet. All west of Warm Creek is pretty much Ballard territory. In between is Lazy Y range, once Bill Yeager's, now yours. If War Hatchet and the Ballards could squeeze out the Lazy Y and tie their holdings together, what would it give them?"

Dave Kerchival stirred restlessly. "All of Mount Cherokee, of course. Slope and top, too. Which would be an empire, sure enough. But you're pointing a long finger, Mel, in a picture where a man has been dry-gulched."

"Call it that if you wish," insisted Rhodes. "Call it anything you want. Though the dry-gulching angle is Joe Orchard's business, and I sure hope he gets his man. But about the rest of it, a man can't blind himself to logic and the obvious."

"We were talking about me," Kerchival reminded him. "Why Bill Yeager picked me."

"And I'm telling you, Dave. Because you know Abel Hendron and how his mind works, better than any other. For that reason you're best suited to hold your own against him. Bill Yeager gave you a ranch, Dave. He also gave you principles to fight for. You're sitting in the saddle of a man who was dry-gulched because he stood in the way of a dream of empire. That's pretty blunt, all right. But this is between you and me, and I'm speaking my honest mind."

Dave Kerchival began building a smoke, his eyes grave and thoughtful. "Once I'm fully sure," he murmured, "I'll speak mine, too."

"Let's go back to logic, Dave," said Rhodes. "Things like this don't just happen. A man might fall off a horse and break his neck. That we could write off as just one of those things . . . fate, hard luck, the mathematics of chance catching up with him. But Bill Yeager was shot out of his saddle. Which rings in the act of another person. And people don't do things of that sort just for the hell of it. They do it because of motive. A man is in their way. They get rid of him. Why?"

Kerchival took a short turn up and down the office. "Damn it, Mel," he growled, "that lawyer mind of yours has a sharp edge to it. It gets inside a thing and cuts and twists until something gives. If Bill Yeager stood in the way of all those things you conjure up, where does it leave me?"

"In the same place Bill was, of course. Which should be a warning to you to sort of ride with your chin on your shoulder and keep off the top of bare ridges, cowboy."

Mel Rhodes broke off to catch up an old magazine and throw it out the office door, where a faint stir of sound had come in the short hall at the head of the stairs.

"Shoo!" he bellowed. Then he explained. "Damned pack rats, Dave. They're taking this whole building over. You ought to be here nights. Sounds like they are running chariot races, upstairs and down. In the store they're driving Sam Liederman half crazy. But to get back to the business about this will. There is some legal procedure to be gone through in Judge Archer's court at Fort Devlin, recordings to be made, and all that sort of thing. I'll take care of all that for you, Dave, and you'll be notified when everything is cleared up. Satisfactory?"

"Sure. Bill me for all the costs. And thanks a lot, Mel."

"For you . . . and Bill Yeager, a pleasure, Dave. And don't you forget for a minute that you're riding in a dead man's saddle."

As he went down the stairs from Mel Rhodes's office, the thought came to Dave Kerchival that he might as well pick up a supply of grub from Sam Liederman, now that he was in town. He had no idea how well Bill Yeager's grub shelf was stocked, back at Lazy Y headquarters. Which was just another of a lot of new angles he was going to have to remember and consider, now that he had an outfit of his own.

Back at War Hatchet, grub was just something a man went into the cook shack and ate, come mealtime. The getting and cooking of it was somebody's affair, but none of his. He wondered, a little wryly, what sort of job he could do of preparing his own grub.

Jack Tully was slouched on his bench beside the store door, sucking on a cold pipe. He looked up as Kerchival came by. "Tough about Bill Yeager, Dave. He was a good man."

"Yes," agreed Kerchival, "a good man. Any other news from the town, Jack?"

A flicker of Tully's sardonic grin showed. "It's said that yesterday afternoon Spence Ballard got buffaloed and that rude and vulgar hands were laid upon Virg Hendron. I been waiting for the stars to fall because of that."

"Long wait, Jack," murmured Kerchival dryly. "The stars don't fall because of the puny affairs of mankind."

Kerchival turned into the store, and Jack Tully, knocking the dottle from his pipe, drifted off downstreet.

In a dark corner of the store Sam Liederman was swearing furiously as he jabbed and banged with a broom handle behind a pile of case goods. Kerchival grinned, and encouraged: "Hit 'em again, Sam."

The storekeeper gave up in disgust, mopping a sweating brow. "Pack rat as big as a coyote," he puffed. "Run right down the length of my counter he did, bristlin' his whiskers at me. I gotta get me a cat, a whole damn' herd of cats, or them cussed rats will take over complete."

"How about a couple of rattlesnakes?" suggested Kerchival, chuckling. "An old-timer back in the hills told me one time that the best rat medicine in the world is a couple of big old rattlers loafing about the premises. The idea suit you, Sam, I'll try and round up a pair for you."

"Rattlesnakes, in my store!" yelped Sam. "You crazy?"

When Kerchival began naming off a list of food items, Liederman looked at him curiously. "I ain't tryin' to run away business, understand, but Lear Hendron and Dusty Elliot were in yesterday gettin' a mess of stuff for War Hatchet. A lot of the same items you're namin', Dave."

"I'm not getting this for War Hatchet, Sam. This is for me."

"What the hell! You going to batch it somewhere?"

"That's right." Kerchival nodded. "Got a ranch of my own now." And then he went on to tell of Bill Yeager's surprising will.

"Be damned!" marveled the storekeeper. "Can you beat that? Havin' a ranch dropped in your lap. Bet you were surprised."

"I'm still fighting my head," admitted Kerchival. "But I'd a mighty lot rather have Bill Yeager alive than own all the ranches in the territory."

"Sure you would, boy," said Liederman soberly. "I know that. Nobody liked Bill Yeager better than me. What a lousy deal he got! Thing like that makes me wonder how come some dirty snakes can walk on two feet. Well, I ain't the sort to rub anybody's back, but I'm here to say that a damn' good man left his ranch to another good one."

A half hour later Dave Kerchival rode out of town, a sack of grub behind his saddle. Also, under his near stirrup fender, was slung a rifle boot, carrying a brand-new Winchester that, as an afterthought, he'd bought from Sam Liederman. He'd shown some hesitation over the act, for it had been a long, long time since he'd ridden with a rifle under his leg. But the grim realities of the past twenty-four hours kept gnawing at him, and the warning words of Mel Rhodes were still strong in his ears. Abruptly, virtually overnight, the Mount Cherokee plateau range had become that kind of a world.

Behind him Kerchival left a town that was still and drowsy in the morning sun. The street was empty, even Jack Tully having disappeared from his favorite post.

Kerchival took his time going home and it was past midday when he again rode up to Lazy Y headquarters. There were no horses standing around now. Brace Shotwell and his riders had pulled out. Kerchival drew up at the corrals, unloaded his sack of grub, unsaddled, and turned his bronco in through the gate bars. Then he just stood, looking around, trying to get the feel of this place and to realize what it was going to mean to him.

It was very still, very peaceful. Here the sun poured in, bright and warming. There the towering sugar pines spread their patterns of shade. A pair of Douglas squirrels set up a chatter, chasing each other around the trunk of a pine. A crested jay swooped overhead on silken wings, a feathered sapphire flashing through the filtered sunlight.

Realization of actual ownership was hard to get hold of, mused Kerchival. It was something he was going to have to get used to. He had ridden so long for the affairs of other men that riding for his own would be a brand-new experience.

Ownership wasn't something you just thought about; it was something you had to feel. It was something that must come up to a man from the earth underfoot, and down from the sky overhead. You wouldn't get it right away and you wouldn't get it easy. You wouldn't get it fully until you had worked and sweated for it, and added something to that which had been given. It was a feeling that would grow and deepen as time went on. It was something to which a man gave strength and fidelity and for which he got unnamed rewards in return. But, in the last analysis, it was something a man had to earn and deserve.

Kerchival was leaning the broad of his shoulders against the corral fence. There was a tiny scurry as a chipmunk came running along the top rail, to stop not a yard away, to sit up and survey Kerchival with bright little eyes, just a tidbit of sleek and vibrant life, little bigger than Kerchival's thumb.

"No, feller," murmured Kerchival softly, "I'm not the one you're looking for. He won't be back. But me and you, we'll get along."

Kerchival shouldered his sack of grub and headed for the cabin. The pile of gear he'd left at the cabin corner early in the morning wasn't in sight. Brace Shotwell and his men had probably put it inside for him before they left.

The cabin door was ajar. Kerchival pushed it wide and stepped through. And then he heard the stir of movement beside him and all his senses shrieked wild warning. It was the sack of grub on his shoulder that was his undoing. It blocked his vision on that side and slowed him just a vital second as he tried to get rid of it and swing around. Something crashed down on his head. The world exploded in a blinding smear of crazy lights, and then he was falling into endless darkness.

CHAPTER FOUR

An air of tension lay over War Hatchet headquarters. After Dave Kerchival rode away, no longer a War Hatchet hand, Dusty Elliot, Perk O'Dair, and Chick Roland puttered around the corrals, greatly busy at doing little or nothing.

"I ain't going to last here very long," announced Chick Roland abruptly. "Feel it in my bones. With Dave gone, I just don't give a thin damn for the layout any more. Somehow I had the feeling before that even though Abel Hendron did sign the pay checks, it was Dave Kerchival I was really working for. But now. . . ." Chick shrugged.

"My sentiments exactly," agreed Perk O'Dair. "Ain't goin' to be the same around here any more . . . ever. I don't feel that I owe Abel Hendron a thing."

Dusty Elliot built a thoughtful cigarette. "For that matter, neither do I," he said gravely. "But Dave said to stay on for a time, so I reckon we will. Maybe Hendron will make up our minds for us. The man's a hard one to figger, but of one thing you can be sure . . . he ain't all fool. He knows how we feel about Dave and, bein' mad at Dave, he may decide to give us our time, too."

"That," declared Chick, "would suit me right down to the ground. He might as well, for I doubt I'll be earning my wages. When my heart ain't in a job, I'm the most useless jigger you ever saw."

"I'm feelin' plenty low about Bill Yeager," said Perk O'Dair soberly. "But as long as nothin' can be done about that, I'm sure glad old Bill willed his layout to Dave. Which, I've a hunch, will still keep the cork in the bottle where the Kingfisher Creek drive trail is concerned. It ain't a pleasant thought to play with, but a feller can't blind himself to the fact that Abel Hendron and those damned Ballards are the only ones who stood to benefit by Bill Yeager's death. Which leads on to. . . ."

"Cut it out, Perk," said Dusty Elliot sharply. "Lay off that line of talk. You don't know a damned thing for sure. Neither does anybody else. And until and unless Joe Orchard comes up with the right answer, don't you go makin' talk that can leave you sittin' right in the middle of a hot griddle."

"A man can't help thinkin'," muttered Perk. "And somebody dry-gulched Yeager."

"Somebody did," agreed Dusty. "But you don't know and I don't know who. And until we do for sure, we're guessin'. And guessin' about a thing like that is unfair and could be dangerous, plenty."

Lear Hendron came out of the ranch house and stood on the kitchen doorstep, shaking a tablecloth. This done, she stood for a moment in the bright pour of the sunlight, staring up at the far crest of the Mount Cherokee rim. Then, with the tablecloth folded over her arm, she turned and went back into the house.

"I don't know how she stands them," observed Chick Roland softly. "Her father and brother, I mean. I think, more than any other reason, that's why I got no use for Abel an' Virg Hendron . . . the way they treat Lear. I can remember when that girl used to laugh and kinda glow with the pure fun of living. Sure, even then she was proud as Punch, but it was a good kind of pride that made you admire her even more than ordinary. But over the past year she's sure changed. She don't laugh no more and the glow is gone. She's still proud, but in a different way, more like she's locking herself away from the world, like she was covering up. That damned overbearing father of hers, and that selfish pup of a brother, they're crushing the life out of her."

Dusty shook himself restlessly. "You and Perk sure give a man the dismals. Let's rake up some work to do. Any kind of work."

"Hold it," said Perk. "Here comes Hendron. Move over, God."

Abel Hendron had stepped out of his office and now came across the interval to the corrals, quick-striding, arrow-straight, coldly austere. "Mister Elliot," he said curtly, "until further notice, you will take over as foreman. Mister Kerchival is no longer in my employ. Your past friendship for him will in no way affect your judgment in relation to your job. First and foremost must come complete and absolute fidelity to the interests of War Hatchet. You will be bound by that fidelity. Needless to say, the same applies to all my other hired hands." His glance touched Perk O'Dair and Chick Roland briefly. "That is all."

He turned and went back as he had come, stiff, unbending, quick of stride.

Perk O'Dair swore softly, pounded a clenched fist on a corral rail. "Just like that. Dave Kerchival is no longer a War Hatchet hand, and Abel Hendron is sore at him. Therefore, Dave should no longer be a friend of ours and we should be sore at him, too. Well, to hell with that. I'll take Dave Kerchival's little finger and somebody else can have Abel Hendron's whole damned arrogant carcass."

"Sometimes," said Chick Roland, "I think that man is crazy. Now I know I'm not going to be around this place very long."

"It ain't goin' to be easy, for a fact," agreed Dusty. "But . . . there's that feed shed that's been needin' some repair. Let's get at it."

They were still at it, hammering and sawing, when, just short of noon, Virg Hendron came riding in. Wherever Virg had been, he hadn't spared his mount any. The claybank gelding was reeking with sweat and badly blown. The slight flush under the eyes that always showed when Virg was packing a little whiskey was there now. He set the claybank back with a heavy hand, stepped from the saddle, and rapped a sharp order at Perk O'Dair.

"Get this saddle off and give the bronc' a rubdown before you corral it, O'Dair!"

For one reason or another—perhaps because he was the youngest of the crew—Virg Hendron seldom seemed to waste a chance to order Perk around. Resentment over this had been building up in Perk for a long time. As a rule, Perk was a cheerful, willing youngster and no trouble hunter. But this had been a rough morning for Perk. To start off with there had been the news of the killing of Bill Yeager, then having Dave Kerchival pull out had upset Perk very considerably. He had been honestly fond of old Bill Yeager, and, because he was still an impressionable kid, his secret feeling toward Kerchival had been one of considerable hero worship. So it was that Virg Hendron had picked the wrong time and place to give Perk another of his curt and domineering orders.

Perk laid down the plank he'd been carrying up to the repair job, looked Virg up and down with a frosty eye, and said flatly: "Unsaddle your own bronc'. Rub him down, too. If you had sense enough to handle a bronc' right, it wouldn't need rubbin' down. Hell with you!"

For a moment Virg Hendron stood stockstill, his chin dropping. He couldn't believe his own ears. O'Dair, a mere hired hand, talking back to him that way! The flush under Virg's eyes spread all over his face. His teeth clicked shut and his lips peeled back. He balled up his fists and started forward. "Why, you two-bit cowhand . . . I'll. . . ."

Perk, with a little whine of eagerness, sighted on Virg's jaw and hit it. Virg staggered, stumbled, and went down.

Dusty Elliot, unable to head off this initial clash because he was balanced on top of a stepladder, groaned with dismay and came scrambling down. As Dusty reached the ground, Chick Roland caught him by the arm.

"Let 'em go, Dusty," said Chick. "It was in the works. It was bound to come. And Perk can't be fired any more for slugging hell out of Virg than he would be for just hitting him once. One more thing . . . if Perk don't lick him, I will."

Virg didn't stay down very long. Momentarily dazed, he pulled up on one elbow, shaking his head. Then, with a thin and menacing curse, he was up and after Perk.

Virg was no taller than Perk, but he was heavier, and supremely confident that he could quickly take apart this red-cheeked, upstart kid rider. But that first smash on the jaw warned him not to get too careless, so he came in with his hands high, feinted Perk out of position, and nailed Perk under the eye with a solid wallop.

Perk's knees buckled slightly, but he did not go down. Virg rushed him, cornered him against the corral fence, and beat furiously at Perk's head with both fists. Perk covered up for a moment, then brought one up inside to the body that made Virg grunt and back up a step. Instantly Perk slammed in a right that made a mess of Virg's mouth.

Chick Roland yelled: "He's soft around the belt, Perk. Work on him there!"

Perk heard, and worked furiously, with both fists. Virg took this punishment while he reached out, clawing, caught hold of Perk, and closed with him. They wrestled back and forth, tripped, and went down in a wild tangle. Here Virg tried to take advantage of his superior weight, but he had an agile, wiry wildcat on his hands in Perk O'Dair. The dust rose, the blood ran, and the fury deepened.

Virg, unable to pin Perk, tried to knee him, at which the wild whine in Perk's throat grew in pitch. Perk got a forearm against his foe's throat and pushed Virg away, strangling and choking. Perk rolled over, bounced to his feet. He was set for Virg when the latter came up, and half hung him across the corral fence with a smash that put a dull glaze over Virg's eyes.

Chick Roland whooped again. "That does it, kid. Now cut him down to size!"

Chick's whoop carried farther than he intended. Abel Hendron came out of his office, stood staring for a moment, then came hurrying. He arrived at the corrals in time to see Perk O'Dair just getting well down to his knitting.

By this time Virg Hendron had had all he wanted of this sort of business. Though a bigger man than Perk, he was now taking a fearful whipping. Things were at work here that had no relation to mere size and weight. In Perk O'Dair lay a young rider who had made his own way through a tough world at a tough trade. And Virg Hendron had been a spoiled son for whom life had been relatively easy. Perk had worked while Virg had loafed. Perk O'Dair was wiry and clean-muscled all through. Deep inside Virg Hendron lay a flabbiness of both flesh and spirit. Virg hadn't ever realized this before, but he knew it now.

Abel Hendron saw all this, too, and the realization turned him gray and shaking with anger. It cut at his pride like bitter acid. He caught at Dusty Elliot's arm and his voice went thin and shrill.

"Stop that thing! Get in there and stop it!"

Dusty, unaware of Abel Hendron's presence until now, automatically started forward just as Perk finished matters with both fists sunk deep into Virg's midriff. Virg collapsed and stayed down, sick and battered.

Perk, wiping a smear of blood from his nose, turned to find Abel Hendron glaring at him, almost incoherent with rage.

"You'd dare!" charged Hendron. "You'd . . . !"

"Yeah," cut in Perk, panting. "I would and I did. I been promisin' myself that pleasure . . . for a long time. While I was at it . . . I got myself a full meal. Funny thing is, I never did like Virg before. But now I do . . . a little. If you hadn't made a spoiled pup outta him, he might have been a man. No, you don't need to say it. I know I'm through. You can make out my time."

With that Perk went over to a horse trough and began mopping away the marks of battle.

Abel Hendron had to have someone upon whom to vent his wrath. He turned to Dusty again. "Why did you allow this thing? You could have stopped it. What kind of a foreman are you? I don't think. . . ."

Revolt rushed out of Dusty. "Stow it," he said wearily. "I've had plenty, too. I'm ridin' with Perk."

"And me," declared Chick Roland. "Make it three of us. You need a different breed of puppy dogs to run your ranch, Hendron."

Perk, wiping water from his face, climbed over the fence and headed for the bunkhouse. Dusty and Chick followed him.

Abel Hendron was a man punching at empty air with his thwarted anger. Virg, hanging onto the fence, was pulling himself slowly erect. His father began to rage at him.

"You . . . a Hendron . . . allowing a common cowhand to do that to you! You quit. You let him whip you . . . beat you down into the dirt. You were afraid. I saw it in your eyes. You! My son. . . ."

Virg hung onto the fence, dropped his head on his arm. "I didn't let him do anything," he blurted thickly. "He just did it. He licked hell outta me. I found out something about myself. I'm soft . . . inside. You made me that way."

Virg came around, facing his father, slowly straightening.

Blood from his battered mouth fanned down his chin. One eye was rapidly closing and his face was swelling and turning dark with bruises. His beaten stomach muscles were shaking uncontrollably. But in his good eye was a light his father had never seen before.

"Yeah, you made me that way," charged Virg again hoarsely. "You made me soft inside. You fed me a lot of guff about Hendron pride. You made me believe that Hendron pride was some kind of a superior thing that a man could ride on all through life. You made me think that being a Hendron was really something. Well, to hell with pride and bully puss. I wish I wasn't a Hendron. I wish I was just an ordinary cowhand, with guts. Like Perk O'Dair."

Having had his say, Virg started to climb the fence. He got over it all right, but he fell down on the other side. He got to his hands and knees, stayed that way a moment, shaking his head. Then he lurched erect and headed for the ranch house, weaving and staggering.

CHAPTER FIVE

There was water on Dave Kerchival's face, water in his throat making him strangle, and there was a pure hell of beating misery in his head. But one way or another he was struggling up out of those black depths. Another douse of water did the trick.

Kerchival opened his eyes, blinked and blinked until things quit spinning and whirling around, and then saw a row of three familiar faces looking down at him anxiously. Dusty Elliot, Chick Roland, and Perk O'Dair. Dusty, holding a tin dipper, was ready for more of the water treatment.

"Leave off," mumbled Kerchival. "Gimme a chance . . . to get my breath. Wh-what happened? My bronc' throw me?"

"If it did," answered Dusty, "it chucked you clear from the corral and plumb through the door. From where I stand, though, I'd say you came off second best in an argument with a gun barrel or a pick handle. You got a knot on your head as big as a potato. Hold still while I pour some more water on it."

Kerchival held still, closing his eyes again. That water on his head felt good now. And it drove some of the stupefying mists away. "I remember now," he murmured. "The door wasn't fully closed and that should have warned me. But I was thinking of something else. . . . Anyhow, they were laying for me, just inside the door. I had a sack of grub on my shoulder and it was in my way. Before I could get rid of it and see who and why, they let me have it. How did you guys happen to come along?"

Dusty shrugged. "Just did. And found you all spread out like

60

a throwed-away dish rag. You were more or less undressed."

"Huh?"

"That's right. Your pockets were turned inside out and your shirt was pulled half off, like somebody had gone over you lookin' for a money belt, or somethin'."

Kerchival struggled to a sitting position on the bunk where he'd been lifted, held his tortured head in his hands for a time, then began fumbling through his rifled pockets.

"What'd they get?" asked Dusty.

"I cashed my pay-off check at Sam Liederman's and spent the big chunk of it for grub and a rifle. There was some left, but that's gone. Did they take my six-shooter?"

"No, it's yonder on the table."

"Well, I'm out about thirty *pesos.* They didn't need to cave my skull in for that measly amount. I'd have given it to them *gratis,* rather than have this head." Kerchival cradled that aching member in his hands again.

"We ain't busted," comforted Dusty. "Perk and Chick and me, we got our pay-off time. And with this stock of grub . . . no, we ain't bad off at all."

Kerchival's head came up again. "We? What are you talking about . . . we?"

For the first time Kerchival took a good look at these three. His glance paused on Perk O'Dair. Perk had a split lip, a black eye, and a satisfied grin.

"Ah," growled Kerchival, "I savvy. Went and got proud, didn't you? Mixed in with Virg Hendron and, by the smug look on your phiz, did a pretty good job for yourself."

"I think I kept the flies off him for a while," admitted Perk cheerfully.

"Did he," chirruped Chick Roland. "I'll say he did. You should have been there, Dave. Done your heart good. Didn't think Perk had it in him, darned if I did. He sure whipped Virg to a peak, and then knocked the peak off. Virg is a wreck. Old man Hendron like to bust a surcingle when he saw the horrible result."

"And of course," said Kerchival dryly, "he right away gave Perk his time."

"He was leading up to it," admitted Chick. "But Perk beat him to it. Perk quit. Which gave me a good out to trail along."

Kerchival grunted. "Darned crazy young jacks. What made up your mind for you?" He looked at Dusty.

Dusty grinned twistedly. "Behold me . . . an ex-foreman. Yes, sir, that's right. I was a foreman for all of four hours. But when Hendron started to pour the rawhide to me because I didn't step in and keep Perk from mussin' up the noble son, I figured I wasn't cut out to be a foreman. So I decided to ride along with Perk and Chick. Which, even though it maybe don't meet with your approval, is still the facts of the case."

Kerchival started to nod, then grabbed his ailing head. "All right . . . all right. So that's how it is and maybe it's just as well. I don't know when I'll be able to pay you three jiggers any wages, or how much. But if you're plumb set on sticking around, I guess I can't kick you off the premises."

"To hell with the wages." Perk grinned. "Me, I allus did want to start from the ground up with a regular outfit. What chores do you want us to start on?"

"Well," answered Kerchival, "this cabin wasn't built to sleep over two men. We'll need more room. Which means another cabin or a bunkhouse. Off the east end of this bench there's a stand of timber about the right size. Soon as this head of mine quiets down a little more, we'll go out there and start cutting logs."

"You ain't goin' nowhere," announced Dusty calmly. "Us three will attend to the log-cuttin'. You stay right on that bunk and take it easy." Dusty turned to Perk O'Dair. "You said you wanted to start from the ground up. Well, here's your chance. That's how we build the new cabin, from the ground up. Let's get at it."

Left alone, Dave Kerchival did nothing for a time but lie quietly, his eyes closed, while the first violent misery in his head faded to a dull ache. He didn't even try to think. Drifting in from the outside came sounds of activity as Dusty and the others put their horses in the corral and made other preparations to stay. He even heard Perk's cheery whistle, a trifle off key because of Perk's split lip.

A certain warmth stole through Kerchival. These three—they were the pure quill, the kind to stick to a friend of their choice through thick and thin, come hell or high water. He might have known that once he left War Hatchet they were bound to leave, too.

Later, sounds in the immediate vicinity of the cabin faded out, but carrying in from the far end of the bench came the measured sound of an axe, the muffled swish and jar of falling timber, and then the drone of a cross-cut saw. Listening to this token of industry and to the steady hum of a bluebottle fly buzzing around somewhere up against the warmth of the cabin roof, Kerchival finally fell asleep.

It was sundown when he awoke, with Dusty tiptoeing about the cabin, getting ready to throw a jag of evening grub together. Kerchival's head felt immeasurably better and he got up and began moving around.

"You know, Dave," said Dusty, over a busy shoulder, "I been thinkin'. Kinda funny that whoever buffaloed you and went through your pockets took only what money you had and left everything else. Now why would they do that?"

"I'll bite," said Kerchival. "Why?"

Dusty scooped some flour into a biscuit pan. "Well, if I was goin' to bat a guy on the head and rob him, I'd more or less take along everything of reasonable value I could lay my hands on. I'd take his six-shooter, his saddle, and other gear that I could peddle somewhere for a few extra dollars. Unless"—and here Dusty paused and blinked thoughtfully—"unless I still aimed to stock around in that same stretch of country where this feller's gun and gear were sure to be recognized by him or some friend of his. All of which adds up to the fact that whoever it was who clouted you is a local character who aims to stay local. He took your money because who's gonna recognize one piece of money from another? But he was plumb careful not to take anything else."

"Maybe there was more than just one of them," said Kerchival.

"One or a dozen," vowed Dusty stoutly, "it adds up to the same answer. And there's somethin' else. If they aimed to get rid of you for the same reason they got rid of Bill Yeager, why didn't they? Why didn't they make sure?"

"Don't try and make me think just now," Kerchival said. "Or my head will start hurting again. I'm plenty satisfied it was no worse than it was."

They ate supper just ahead of dusk, then sat outside and smoked. "This layout," said the impressionable Perk, "sure gets into a man's blood. All easy and quiet and peaceful. A man can sure ease down here and let his edges sink into the ground. Right now I couldn't be mad at anybody."

"Not even Virg Hendron?" gibed Chick Roland.

"Nope, not even Virg. Funny thing there, like I told old man Hendron. When I started in on Virg, I was ready to eat him alive, but, toward the end, darned if I didn't feel sorry for him."

Dusty grunted dryly. "You sure had a hell of a queer way of showin' him how sorry you was. You were wallopin' him twice as hard at the finish as you were at the start."

"Shucks," retorted Perk defensively, "it was kinder that way. I didn't want to drag it out. You and Chick are knot-heads, Dusty, but I bet Dave understands what I mean."

"I think I do, Perk," said Kerchival gravely. "It must be tough to have to live under the same roof with Abel Hendron."

With only two bunks in the cabin, Perk and Chick made out that night on a hay pile in a feed shed. And with a solid night of sleep under his belt, Dave Kerchival arose the next morning feeling pretty much his old self. His head was sore and tender, but the ache was gone.

Immediately after breakfast Dusty and Perk and Chick headed out for further log-cutting, while Kerchival took stock inside. There was an old cigar box on the grub shelf and in this were the frugal records Bill Yeager had kept. There were a couple of dog-eared tally books, and a quick study of these told Kerchival that there were a little better than six hundred head of cattle grazing the slope range carrying the Lazy Y brand. Besides the tally books there were a couple of paid-up notes, several years old, drawn by the Cattleman's Mercantile Bank in Fort Devlin, and there was a checkbook on the same bank showing a balance of a trifle under $8,000.

Again the realization of ownership was difficult to grasp. What these records showed was his. His—Dave Kerchival's. Bill Yeager had given it all to him. The final act of a man who lay dying. These records and figures added up to the sum total of a good man's effort in life. Dollars earned through toil and hardship and dogged purpose, and as carefully saved, eight thousand of them. And cattle, a herd of six hundred head. One man's modest wealth, amassed without ever using the neck of another man as a steppingstone. A broad range, a part of the giving earth, bought and held by this same toil and purpose, and finally paid for with a life snuffed out by a cowardly bullet.

Good range, with tall trees to give it majesty, sweet water to nourish it, and rich grass to cover it—these things Bill Yeager had given to him. And now Dave Kerchival knew beyond all doubt that Yeager had given him something more. A purpose. As Kerchival put the records carefully away again, he murmured softly: "OK, Bill. I won't let you down."

Kerchival went out and saddled up, then rode out to where Dusty and Perk and Chick were toiling. "I'm going to ride a little circle and see how Lazy Y cows are doing. Later I'll help you at this chore."

Dusty came around Kerchival's horse and saw that Kerchival had his rifle slung to his saddle. Dusty dropped a hand on the stock of the weapon.

"That's right," he said grimly. "Keep it with you all the time, Dave. Don't ever forget you're ridin' in a dead man's saddle."

It was the same expression Mel Rhodes had used. Kerchival nodded. "Since walking into that bust on the head, I ain't liable to forget."

He rode leisurely, swinging west as far as Warm Creek, then turning upslope toward the rim, then east to Kingfisher, and finally down along that hurrying creek's west bank. He saw cattle. Lazy Y cattle. His cattle. They fed or rested along the swelling rolls of the great slope, or in hollows and basins and in the big meadows through the timber. He saw them filing in to water along the creeks. Fat cattle. This chunk of graze could handle twice the number of head that now used it, and with the summer range on the plateau top beyond the rim, well—a man could build here if his mind ran that way.

Along the way Kerchival did a lot of thinking about other things than cattle and range. Particularly did he go back to the mysterious attack on him, going over every item of it he could recall, trying to flush out some sort of answer. Simple robbery still seemed the most logical answer, else why had he been left alive? Nor did it mean that Dusty Elliot's theory of its being pulled by some local character was necessarily correct.

Rather, it could have been some drifter, perhaps some wanted man who had come in across Mount Cherokee, broke and hungry, and who had merely added one more misdeal in a deal already thoroughly bad. That the fellow had taken nothing more than the few dollars in Kerchival's pocket was no definite proof of anything, either. Probably the fellow already owned all the guns he wanted to pack, and maybe his saddle was a better one than the one Kerchival sat in. The more he thought about it, the more Kerchival decided that it was just one of those things, to be written off and let lie.

Both Mel Rhodes and Dusty Elliot had warned him that he rode in a dead man's saddle, which was true enough. But if they had killed Bill Yeager, why hadn't they killed him, instead of just knocking him on the head and looting his jeans of a few dollars? And who would *they* be? Hardly the Ballards. For they would not have stopped at merely buffaloing him, once they had him helpless and at their mercy. No matter how he looked at it, the only logical answer seemed to be that of a chance drifter.

Here Kingfisher Creek broke through a little gorge, plunging steeply for a short hundred yards. The tumult of the tumbling water smothered all other sound. It was not until the quick-dropping trail leveled out again at the foot of the gorge that Kerchival became aware of another rider, and then it was his horse's quick-swinging head and short, gusty nicker that warned him. He came around in his saddle, hard and taut, hand streaking for his gun. He caught the move halfway, feeling foolish. The rider was Lear Hendron. Her horse was drinking at the long, shining riffle below the gorge. She was looking at him, grave and quiet.

Chapter Six

Dave Kerchival reined down the short, sharp bank, sent his horse splashing across the riffle, and pulled up beside Lear Hendron. She was bareheaded, dressed in a divided skirt of gray whipcord and a silk blouse that set off her slim shoulders and the warmly suntanned curve of her throat. There was an unsmiling stillness about her as she met his eyes.

"Lear," he said, "I'm glad to see you, for I've been wanting to tell you something. I don't know where the happenings of the last two or three days leave you and me, and I don't know if you're even slightly interested. But I want you to know that the lone regret I had in leaving War Hatchet was you."

A recklessness was suddenly running loose in him, a certain sense of freedom. Before he'd been a War Hatchet hand, a hired man, and bound to certain decorum of action and word by that fact. Now he was his own man, a cattleman in his own right, free to speak his mind to any and all.

"Many times," he went on, "I was near to blowing up, to pulling the pin, asking for my time. But I'd think of you and then'd hang on. For it meant a great deal to be near you, to see you about the house and ranch, to speak to you now and then. I wanted you to know that."

Her eyes fell away, rested on the sliding, shining water. A faint wave of color washed up her throat and face. Still she was silent, and for so long that the warm spirit faded out of Dave

Kerchival's eyes and face and a clouded remoteness took its place.

"I see," he said. "I understand. I'm sorry I bothered you. I keep forgetting that the Hendron blood. . . ."

"Don't say that." Her eyes were back on him and the look in them made him wince. It was almost as though he'd hit her with a whip. "No," she cried again, "don't say that! That's why you find me out here, riding. To get away from being reminded about my Hendron blood and the Hendron name and . . . and all things Hendron. You . . . you don't see, and you don't understand. Nobody does."

Her glance moved back to the water and she was silent again. Her hands were folded on her saddle horn, slim brown hands, with the knuckles showing white with tension. Kerchival said nothing, building a cigarette. Her head was bent a little forward, and a tendril of hair, tugged loose by riding, lay down the curve of her cheek. She looked very girlish and somehow forlorn. Presently she began to speak, her voice low and full.

"I used to ride this way, often. To see him, Bill Yeager. In a way he was a refuge from . . . from things at home. He was so kind and understanding. He saw that there was so much more to life than just cattle and range and endless, fanatic yearning and scheming and planning on how to get more cattle and more range. So much more than driving, driving, driving to be bigger, more powerful, more arrogant than anyone else. I . . . I don't know how I could have carried on if it hadn't been for Bill Yeager and the comfort of his understanding.

"We used to sit out under the sugar pines at Lazy Y headquarters and talk. The Douglas squirrels would come down and climb on his knee and take food from his fingers. Chipmunks would go through his pockets for tidbits. His horses would stand at the corral fence and nicker at him until he went over and petted them. There was a great and understanding sweetness in old Bill Yeager. And . . . and they killed him. They killed a man like that. . . ."

Her voice ran off into choked silence. She dug a wisp of handkerchief from the pocket of her blouse, dabbed at her eyes with it. She swallowed once or twice, then went on.

"It was such a relief to come and see him, to listen to him talk in his low, kind way. To . . . to get away from stupid pride, from blind, selfish arrogance, and unbending authority. To get away from a house and ranch run like a military parade, where it is almost a crime to laugh or to sing. From being constantly reminded that the Ballards are my cousins and that I must be nice to them. When I hate them . . . hate them! The Ballards . . . with their bombast and blow and slinking wolf ways!"

A wild, almost hysterical note came with the mounting vehemence of her words. Then she caught herself abruptly and went quiet again.

Dave Kerchival was startled, astounded by this girl's outburst. For the first time since he had known her she had let him see past the wall of her pride, let him glimpse her true thoughts and emotions. He could think of nothing to say. But a great pity for her rode within him. In her words and tone he glimpsed something of the staggering loneliness that had been and still was so large a part of her life.

A lone girl in a world of cattle and men. Living in a house bludgeoned and subdued by the unbending, self-centered, austere spirit and authority of Abel Hendron. Virtually no social life, not even a trip down to an occasional dance in Warm Creek any more. Surrounded by fetters she could not break yet against which she was in constant rebellion. Yearning for the simple brightness of life, which was denied her by the chill mists of Abel Hendron's obsessions. And, until now, hiding all this behind a facsimile of her father's unyielding formality.

Abruptly she swung her horse away from the creek, urged it a few yards up the bank. There she paused and looked back at Kerchival, her eyes wetly shining, her lips showing just the slightest quiver. She had courage, this girl.

"Thank you for listening to me, Dave. I did not expect to meet you here and I never dreamed I would say all I have. But something seemed to unlock. I'm glad you said what you did. I think I have known it, for a long time. But I was glad to hear you say it. Now . . . you must be careful. You must remember what they did to . . . to Bill Yeager."

With that she was swiftly gone, lifting her horse to a run, flashing past the alders and willows and away across the far slope.

Dave Kerchival rode back to headquarters, soberly thoughtful. He put up his horse, went over to the end of the bench land, and helped Dusty and Perk and Chick cut logs for the new bunkhouse. He worked hard, feeling the sweat run down his face and throat and chest. He swung his axe with a sort of bitter vehemence, thinking of Lear Hendron as she had sat there by the singing creek shallows, giving up to him the confidences she had so long concealed. Thinking of Bill Yeager and of the Ballards, and finally thinking of a cold, unbending, precise man with skin like a woman's and brown eyes as hard and masking as two pieces of bottle glass. Of Abel Hendron.

He came close to overdoing, for a dull ache began to build up in his beaten head by the time the day ran out and sunset mists were like powder-blue smoke, coiling through the sugar pines. When they knocked off work and went back to the cabin, it was Joe Orchard who came riding, leading a gaunt horse with an empty saddle.

"Found this bronco with its reins tangled in some jack pines off the west side of the town trail," explained the deputy. "Heard the animal nicker when I was riding by. I make it the one Bill Yeager was shot off. It must've spooked and run at the shot.

When Bill came to, he didn't have any bronco, so he headed for town afoot and made it, though he was dying all the time. The saddle has been on this bronco plenty long, so its back will need care."

Perk and Chick took over the care of the horse, and Dusty went in to start supper. Joe Orchard asked Kerchival: "What are those three boys doing here? Don't tell me Abel Hendron made you a loan of them."

"Hardly," retorted Kerchival dryly. He told of the circumstances leading up to Dusty and Perk and Chick's leaving War Hatchet. Then he asked: "You have any luck, Joe?"

The deputy shook his head. He was weary and gaunt and pinched from hard riding and little rest. "Nothing I can prove. I made a call on the Ballards an' put them over the jumps. They acted righteous as hell, of course. I couldn't get a thing on them, but I had the queer feelin' that they were laughing at me all the time. I wouldn't say they had anything to do with Bill Yeager's dry-gulching, and I wouldn't say they didn't . . . yet. Say, boy, you look a little peaked yourself. What's wrong?"

Kerchival told him the whole story. How he had found Brace Shotwell and the plains riders here at the cabin, how he and Shotwell had gone to town to see Bill Yeager's will, of his own return, and of the surprise attack and rifling of his pockets.

"I've got no idea who, and damned little idea why, Joe. But I got this sore head to remind me it sure enough happened. Dusty's got a theory and maybe he's right. But somehow it doesn't add up for me."

"What's Dusty think?" asked Joe Orchard.

"He figures it was some local character who was broke and figured that by rapping me on the head and going through my pockets he'd end up well heeled. Which, if true, must have been quite a disappointment to that particular *hombre*." Kerchival smiled crookedly. "Dusty figured it was some local rider, because he took only the money, not touching anything else . . . like my gun or other gear."

"Ain't such bad reasoning, at that," said the deputy. "No chance of money being identified, but anything else could be recognized. Big hole in Dusty's theory is . . . how'd this jigger know whether you had fifty dollars or fifty cents in your jeans?"

"Well," said Kerchival, "for that matter I had just been paid off at War Hatchet."

Joe Orchard pinched a pursed lower lip between thumb and forefinger, then shook his head. "Uhn-uh. Still don't add up. A cowhand ain't exactly a rich man just because he's been paid off. Leastways, none I ever met was. But say he had proof in his pocket that he owned a cattle ranch that somebody else didn't want him to own . . . ?" Joe left this supposition hanging in the air.

"You're speaking of Bill Yeager's will, of course," mused Kerchival. "Well, I did think of that, too. But I'd hardly be packing a thing like that around loose and careless, would I? Besides which, being just drawn, it would have to be presented and passed on in a proper court, recorded, and all that sort of legal business. They'd know that."

"Um . . . mebbe. But not necessarily." Joe Orchard scrubbed a weary hand across his brow. "From what I've seen of 'em, the average guy is plenty ignorant about legal things. Me, I know a little about the law, but what I don't know would fill a damn' big book. Yet alongside of most I'm a walking encyclopedia. More I think of it, the more I believe it was the will they were after."

"Who would *they* be, Joe?"

"Who can say? The Ballards, mebbe. Or even Abel Hendron, or somebody working for him."

"That would be tying them in with the killing of Bill Yeager, Joe."

"What of it? Somebody killed him, and they didn't do it for fun," said the deputy dryly. "There's a lot of mixed-up trails, but somewhere in the mess is the right one, and, sooner or later, I'll work it out."

They went in and had supper, after which Kerchival got down the cigar box and showed Joe Orchard the frugal records Bill Yeager had kept. They talked these over for a while. Joe Orchard sprawled on one of the bunks, resting and smoking. Of a sudden, the deputy began to snore.

"Joe ain't as young as he used to be," observed Dusty Elliot softly. "He's been poundin' the saddle steady and is plumb tuckered. Cover him up and leave him there, Dave. I'll make out for the night in the hay with Perk and Chick."

For a long time before falling asleep Dave Kerchival lay, wide-eyed and thoughtful, on the other bunk. He thought about Bill Yeager; he thought about the will. He went back carefully over every single happening that had taken place since his return from the Fort Devlin country. And he was still left without an answer that was concrete. In the end he thought of Lear Hendron. In what she had said at their meeting along Kingfisher Creek, she had spoken of *they*, just as Joe Orchard had. They? Maybe the Ballards—maybe her own father—maybe her father and the Ballards working together. Kerchival stirred restlessly. Whatever the darkening future brought, he hoped Lear Hendron wouldn't be hurt too much.

It was black dark when Kerchival awoke, and he could hear Joe Orchard stirring, too. Dusty Elliot was calling at the cabin door: "Get out here, Dave. Get out here! Bring Joe Orchard with you. He's wanted!"

Kerchival threw his blankets aside, fumbled for the lamp, and got it going. He and Joe Orchard hurried out, and the deputy called: "What is it, Dusty?"

"It's Bus Spurgeon, from town. He's got something to tell you."

The owner of the livery barn in Warm Creek was a humped shape on a hard-panting horse there in the chill, pallid star gleam.

"All right, Bus," growled Joe Orchard. "Let's have it. What's wrong?"

"Sam Liederman sent me out to find you, Joe," mumbled the livery owner. "I been blunderin' all over hell-and-gone through these damn' hills. I took a chance that you might be here. You're wanted in town right away. Mel Rhodes . . . he's dead!"

"Dead! Mel Rhodes?"

"That's right. Somebody stuck a knife in him an' robbed the safe in his office."

Through the lifeless early morning hours they stormed down the black slope toward town. Dave Kerchival, Joe Orchard, Dusty Elliot, and Bus Spurgeon. At Kerchival's order, Perk O'Dair and Chick Roland stayed on at Lazy Y headquarters.

During the flurry of catching and saddling, Bus Spurgeon had given brief details. It was, it seemed, the habit of Sam Liederman and Mel Rhodes to meet of an evening with Hack Dinwiddie at the latter's Starlight Hotel for a session of pinochle. This night Mel Rhodes had begged off, saying he had some work to catch up on. So Liederman had rounded up Bus Spurgeon to take Rhodes's place.

When Liederman and Spurgeon went up to the Starlight, there was a light burning in the lawyer's office. When the pinochle game broke up around 11:00 and Liederman and Spurgeon headed back to their respective sleeping quarters, that light was still burning. So they decided to go on up and invite Rhodes over to the Rialto with them for a nightcap.

They found Mel Rhodes lying face down beside his desk,

stabbed to the heart. His safe door was swung wide and legal papers of one sort or another were scattered all over the place.

Various citizens had been routed out and sent riding in search of Joe Orchard, one of these being Bus Spurgeon. Bus had tried Lazy Y headquarters and that was that.

A still cold rage lay all through Dave Kerchival, for the moment overshadowing his grief at losing as fine a friend as Mel Rhodes had been. First Bill Yeager and now Mel Rhodes. No two better men had ever walked the earth than these. Both had been foully done to death, one by a dry-gulcher's cowardly slug, the other by an equally cowardly knife in the back. Why? And by whom?

It was a question that was beginning to tower in Kerchival's consciousness like some great black thunderhead turning its chill shadow over the world. He might guess at the answers, but what did he know? He ground his teeth at the nagging futility of it.

Town had never seemed so far away, but they beat into it finally, racing through the dark. A light was on in Mel Rhodes's office, and in there Sam Liederman and Hack Dinwiddie and Doc Cable were holding vigil over a dead friend and his rifled office.

Hack Dinwiddie was somberly grim. Doc Cable was pacing up and down. Sam Liederman was hunkered down against a far wall. The fat little storekeeper's face was frankly streaked with tears. He was humped and crushed. Mel Rhodes's body was covered with a blanket.

Joe Orchard turned to Doc Cable, who said: "I disturbed him as little as possible, Joe, knowing you'd want to see him exactly as he was found. One deadly thrust to the heart. The angle of the wound shows that it was struck from behind. Death must have been instantaneous . . . or almost so. Probably he never even saw the one who killed him."

Joe Orchard stripped the blanket aside and looked matters over, face grim and expressionless. Presently he nodded and said: "You can take him away now, Doc."

Dusty Elliot, Hack Dinwiddie, and Bus Spurgeon helped Doc carry the body away. Joe Orchard dropped a kindly hand on Sam Liederman's shoulder and told him to get some rest. Sam got to his feet, shuffled to the door, then paused.

"I got a little money, Joe. You can have it all, just so you get the one who did this and see him hung."

"Knowing how you feel, Sam, I won't hold those words against you. But I'm reminding you that Mel Rhodes was a damned good friend of mine, too." Joe Orchard snapped his fingers. "Go on. Get some rest. You can't do any good here."

When the storekeeper was gone, Joe closed the door and said to Dave Kerchival: "Now we can start looking. But it's sure to be gone."

They gathered up and went over carefully every scrap of paper in the office. Bill Yeager's will was not among these. Joe Orchard said wearily: "It's open and shut what they came after, and it looks like they got it."

"So now we come back to *they* again," said Dave Kerchival harshly. "It's like talking about shadows. Pretty soon, Joe, we've got to put that tag definitely against somebody and then do something about it."

"It ain't what I'd like to do," said the deputy bitterly. "It's what I can prove. That's the way the law has to work, Dave. I can suspect from here to hell-and-gone, but, unless I can back that up with some sort of proof, my hands are tied. I'll be doing all I can, of course."

"So will I. And my hands won't be tied. Joe, I'm going to start getting rough. One thing, this just about supplies the answer to why I was clouted over the head and my pockets rifled. It was that will they were after. When they found I didn't have it on me, they figured it would be here in Mel's safe. So they made another try. But why in God's name should they kill poor Mel and only part my hair for a time? The will named me owner of Lazy Y, not Mel."

Joe Orchard dropped into the desk chair and nursed his stubby pipe as though it brought him vast comfort at the moment. "Could have been that Mel saw 'em and they had to kill him to close his mouth. Mebbe they'd dropped in here and were talking with Mel on some excuse or another, and then jumped him when his back was turned. That's a pretty good safe of Mel's yonder. Once it was closed and locked, it couldn't be busted into without raising a hell of a clatter that could have stirred up somebody around town and brought 'em investigating. Without knowin' the combination of the safe, a man would have had to use plenty of cold chisel an' sledge-hammer work, or a charge of dynamite. But if he was to drop in sort of casual-like, to shoot the breeze with Mel, knowing Mel usually kept the safe open until he left for the night. . . ."

Dave Kerchival nodded somberly, finishing Joe's thought for him: "And seeing that the safe was open, he waited until Mel was off guard, then used the knife. Which would keep things quiet and not stir up an alarm and allow for a safe getaway. Joe, that's about it."

"I think so," said Joe. "It'll do until a better guess comes along."

Kerchival built a cigarette, staring harsh-eyed at nothing. "Maybe they got that will, and then again, maybe they didn't. Maybe Mel had already mailed it off to Judge Archer's court at Fort Devlin to be put through all the necessary legal hocus-pocus."

"That could be so," admitted Joe. "Mebbe we can find out for sure. There's nothing we can do here but lock up. Let's go catch Sam Liederman before he turns in. I want to ask him a question."

Sam Liederman was a bachelor, with living quarters out back of his store. Kerchival and the deputy went around back and saw a light burning. Joe Orchard's knock brought the storekeeper shuffling to the door, lamp held high.

"Sorry to bother you again, Sam," said Orchard. "But Dave and me are trying to figure a few angles and mebbe you can help us on one. Won't keep you long. When you went up early in the evening to try and get Mel Rhodes to go over to the Starlight with you for that pinochle game that you and Hack Dinwiddie and Mel generally had of evenings, Mel begged off because he had some work to do. That's right, ain't it?"

Sam nodded, his round, ruddy face creased with misery. "I should have made him go along with me. Then he'd be alive now. I'll always remember that and always blame myself."

"No point in blaming yourself, Sam. Not your fault," said Joe Orchard. "What I'm wondering is this. When Mel begged off from the pinochle game, did he give any reason why he was working late? Did he mention having anybody due in to talk business with of some kind?"

Sam shook his head. "No, Mel didn't say anything about that. He said he had to make a trip out to Fort Devlin on business and he wanted to get some odds an' ends of office work cleaned up before he left."

"Thanks, Sam. That helps a lot. That's what Dave and me wanted to know. Good night, Sam."

They circled slowly back to the street. "That settles it," said Kerchival. "They got the will. That's why Mel figured on a trip to Fort Devlin . . . to handle the will business. Well, that will was the only legal proof of ownership of Lazy Y that I could fall back on. Now it's gone, and whoever takes Lazy Y and holds it will keep on holding it. Right now I got it . . . and I'll keep it."

"That's the way Bill Yeager intended it," admitted Joe Orchard.

"Something else," Kerchival growled. "If anybody should try and move in on Lazy Y, it will be just about admitting they got the will . . . or that they know I ain't got it. Which ties them in on Mel Rhodes's murder. Bill Yeager's, too."

"Good theory," grunted the deputy, "but it still leaves us punching at nothing. Just suppose it was Abel Hendron who tried to move in. Could you go up to him and say . . . 'Hendron, you killed Mel Rhodes?' You might say as much, Dave, but he could laugh in your face and dare you to prove it. Should the Ballards try and move in and you went up to any one of them with the same accusation, they could offer you the same dare. And where would that leave you? Dave, you got to remember that thinking is one thing, while proving is something else again."

Kerchival swore softly. "Joe, it's like having your hands tied with ropes you can't see but that you can't cut, either."

"You're telling me!" exclaimed the deputy.

"Of course I still got one angle," Kerchival said. "Both you and Doc Cable are living witnesses that Bill Yeager drew a will. You could swear to that in court and you could swear to what the will said."

"We could, and would be glad to," admitted Joe Orchard dryly. "Which still wouldn't mean a damned thing. Without the actual will to go on the only thing the court could do would be declare that Bill Yeager died intestate. After that, the tangle could drag on and on until you'd be an old gray-headed man. The only sound thing left for you to do is just what you said you were going to. Hang onto Lazy Y against any and all comers until something breaks. Until I can mebbe turn up something real and solid to go on. It's still a blind trail and a tough one, but I've just started riding it."

Abruptly Kerchival realized that Warm Creek was no longer a town deep-shrouded with earth's shadowed blackness. The bulk of buildings seemed to lift and grow and their roofs' corners and edges grow sharper against a graying light. Dawn was at hand.

Kerchival went in search of Dusty Elliot.

CHAPTER SEVEN

After Dave Kerchival and Dusty Elliot rode away from Lazy Y headquarters with Joe Orchard and Bus Spurgeon, there was no chance of further sleep that night for Perk O'Dair and Chick Roland. Both were young and both were impressionable. And the dark news that Bus Spurgeon had brought left them restless and troubled. They did not go back to their blankets in the hay, but instead took over in the cabin, building up the fire and cooking a pot of coffee, of which they drank numerous cups while they sat and smoked and talked in subdued tones under the yellow light of the cabin lamp.

Both Perk and Chick knew Mel Rhodes and liked him, as did most men who had known the lawyer. It was hard to face the cold fact that he was gone, done to death as foully as Bill Yeager had been.

"It all ties up with this cabin we're sitting in, Perk," said Chick Roland. "And something tells me it's only the beginning. I'm still wondering how it happened that whoever it was that buffaloed Dave didn't kill him, too. Seems to be the fashion around here. Killing a man from behind, I mean."

"For a long time it was a pretty good range," said Perk gloomily. "Now, all of a sudden, it's turned bad. A feller hears talk of this sort of thing happenin' on ranges where he's never been and it sounds sort of excitin' and interestin'. But when it jumps up and hits you in the face, and it's good men and friends like Mel Rhodes and Bill Yeager who get it, why, then you see it for what it really is. You see it as mean and dirty, and it leaves you all cold and empty-like inside. Chick, did you ever throw a gun on a man?"

"No," declared Chick, "and I never want to, unless not doing it leaves me feeling that I can't live with myself any more. Of course, a man never knows. Particularly the way things are shaping up around here. Could come a time, mebbe, when a feller just wouldn't have any other out, when it'd be jest a case of shoot or be shot. Then I reckon I'd have the moxie to go through with it. I hope so."

Perk nodded soberly. "That's the way I feel, exactly. I sure hope I never have to, but if it means I have to leave Dave Kerchival down by not doin' it . . . why, then I'll do it. I'll throw my gun an' do my darnedest with it."

So they talked while the morning's black hours ran away and a new day began peering through the cabin windows, making the lamplight glow small and futile. Then they set about cooking up some breakfast and were sitting down to it when there came a faint stir at the doorway. Right after that sounded the hard, uncompromising order: "Just stay right like you are! Any queer moves and you get it!"

Perk and Chick swung startled heads and looked into the muzzle of a gun held by Gard Ballard. At Gard's shoulder, ready to back him up if any rough play started, was his brother Spence. Spence had a hungry, wicked glint in his black eyes, as though he hoped Perk and Chick would make something of this.

Gard Ballard made a little motion with his gun barrel. "Put your hands on top of your heads, get up, and come over here."

There was nothing Perk and Chick could do but obey. Spence Ballard stepped past Gard and took their guns. Spence snarled at them: "Over against that wall and stay there!"

Gard called over his shoulder: "All right, Turk! You and the other boys can come in now."

He walked over and faced Chick and Perk. "Where's Kerchival and Elliot? Speak up."

"Town," answered Chick.

"They must've left damn' early," cut in Spence. "Why?"

"They did. Right after midnight."

"Don't lie to me," rapped Spence viciously, "or I'll knock your teeth in. Nobody heads for town in the middle of the night without good reason."

"They had good reason," retorted Chick, jaw going tight under Spence's rough tongue. "They went in with Joe Orchard. Somebody had knifed Mel Rhodes to death. Bus Spurgeon brought the word."

Perk, saying nothing as yet, was watching Gard and Spence closely. He saw the startled widening of their eyes at Chick's words.

"Rhodes . . . knifed?" Gard's words were sharp and high.

"That's what Bus Spurgeon said."

"Who did it?"

Chick shrugged. "You guess. I wouldn't know."

Before Gard could ask any more questions, the youngest Ballard, Turk, came in, followed by four other riders, all of these strangers to Chick and Perk. To them Gard said: "We drew it easy. Only these two around. Kerchival and Elliot are in town."

"And with coffee cookin'," said one of the strange riders. "Which smells good to me. How's for a cup?"

Turk Ballard swaggered over to Perk O'Dair. "Understand you whipped hell outta Virg Hendron," Turk taunted. "Which don't exactly hurt my feelin's. Yet I'm sure my dear cousin would want me to do this for him."

Turk rolled his shoulder and drove a clenched fist into Perk's face. It was a cowardly and unexpected blow, and it slammed Perk back into the wall. Perk bounced back, dropped his hands, and would have torn into Turk like a mad catamount, then and there, but Chick's yell cut through the white rage that had engulfed Perk.

"Hold it, Perk! You can't win against this set-up. Hold it, boy!"

Perk managed to do so. He was pallid and shaking with fury, but he held up, scrubbing the back of a hand across his bleeding mouth. Turk acted as if he might throw another punch, but Gard cut him short.

"Lay off! That's not what we're here for. And it didn't take much guts. Try it again and I turn O'Dair loose on you . . . with an even break. Might teach you somethin'."

"That," mumbled Perk hoarsely, "I'd love. Just say the word, Ballard."

Spence Ballard said: "Shut up, O'Dair. Nobody's talkin' to you. What you goin' to do with 'em, Gard?"

"Send 'em packin'." Gard looked at Perk and Chick. "Go out, get your broncs, and scatter. Go tell Kerchival if you want. Tell him we've taken over and that we stay put. Tell him that, if he or Elliot or either of you two show up around here again, you'll probably stay here for good. That's all. Get gone!"

Ten minutes later Perk O'Dair and Chick Roland were spurring for town. Perk looked back once. "Remember what we were talkin' about, Chick? About throwin' a gun on a man? I've changed my mind. I can't wait."

CHAPTER EIGHT

Dave Kerchival and Dusty Elliot were having breakfast at the A-1 Café when the door pushed open and in came Perk O'Dair and Chick Roland. Kerchival, throwing them a narrowed glance, saw that the two young riders were seething with a shamed fury. He saw also that Perk's mouth showed fresh signs of fistic activity.

"Thought I told you two to stick around headquarters," said Kerchival brusquely. "Or did you decide to go off and get ambitious again?" He looked directly at Perk.

Perk met the look squarely. "We ain't fit to stand guard over a cage of chipmunks, Dave. They sure made suckers outta us."

Here it is again, thought Kerchival. *They.* He growled: "I'm listening."

"We were mixin' up some breakfast. Next thing we knew they were comin' through the door, throwin' guns on us. We never had a chance. They told. . . ."

"Who," cut in Kerchival harshly, "were they?"

"The Ballards and four others, strangers to Chick and me. They took our guns away, backed us up against a wall, and started askin' questions. Wanted to know where you an' Dusty were. When we told 'em you were in town, they wanted to know what time you left. We told 'em it was a little past midnight, and then they wanted to know why."

"You told them about Mel Rhodes?"

"Yeah. Didn't make sense not to."

86

"No, it wouldn't have," admitted Kerchival. "Don't tell me they were surprised at the news."

"If they weren't, they were damn' good actors," declared Perk. "I was thinkin' just what you're thinkin', so I watched Gard and Spence Ballard plenty close while Chick was tellin' 'em. And if they weren't damn' well surprised, then they sure put on a mighty good show of bein'."

Kerchival considered this for a moment, then said: "How come you got walloped? You must have sassed them some for one of them to take a wallop at you."

Fury seethed in Perk anew. "I never made a single wrong move. It was Turk. He jest stepped up, made some crack about doin' this for Virg Hendron, then let me have one. Gard kinda ground him down for that. Anyhow, they took our guns away from us, told us to saddle up, and get the hell out. Said that they were takin' over and that we could locate you and tell you so. Kinda as a snapper to the whip, Gard said, if you or Dusty or us showed around there again, we ran a good chance of stayin' permanent. That's a bet Chick and me would sure like to call."

Kerchival sat silently for a moment, swirling the last mouthful of coffee in his cup before downing it. He was still silent as he began spinning a cigarette into shape. Perk and Chick squirmed under what they read as his complete disgust with them, and Chick, unable to hold in any longer, blurted his misery.

"Damn it, Dave, no matter how bad you feel, Perk and me feel worse. We let you down and we feel lower than the belly of a snake in a wagon track."

Kerchival smiled crookedly at them. "Cheer up. You didn't let anybody down under those conditions. It was my fault more than yours. I should have foreseen something like this and put you on your guard more . . . let you know what might happen."

He inhaled deeply and his face pulled into raw, hard angles. "Well, this is it. The lid's off and I'm ready to go just as far as the other side, and probably farther. Still willing to trail along with me?"

"Through hellfire!" vowed the two together eagerly.

"All right. Go over to Sam Liederman's and get yourselves some new guns. Tell Sam to charge them to me. After that, head for the Ballard headquarters over west. Don't go in directly. Check things out carefully and see who they've left there, if anybody. When you're sure, come back as quiet as you went, and see me here in town."

Kerchival turned to Dusty Elliot. "You hit for the plains, cowboy. Get hold of Brace Shotwell and Joe Kirby. Tell them what's happened. Tell them we've lost possession of Lazy Y, but that we're going to get it back . . . the rough way if necessary. Tell them we'd appreciate their help, along with eight or ten of their hands who know how to use a gun and are tough enough not to back away from powder smoke."

"Good enough," said Dusty. "And what are you goin' to do?"

Kerchival's eyes pinched down at the corners and his lips flattened to a straight line. "Why, I'm going to declare myself, here and there. It's become that kind of a set-up. Be careful, all of you. Don't take anything for granted."

The sun was up when Kerchival went back to the street. Gil Lambie swung his stage away from Bus Spurgeon's livery corrals and drove up to the Starlight, where Hack Dinwiddie came out and spoke to him briefly. Then Gil brought his team around in a sweeping, trace-jangling turn, and lined out for the Fort Devlin road, lifting his whip slightly in greeting to Kerchival as the Concord lumbered past. A haze of dust lifted, hung, then settled.

Jack Tully appeared, moving in his stumpy, leisurely way, and settled down on his favorite spot on the bench beside Sam Liederman's door, where the slanting sun struck fully. Dave Ker-chival, spinning a cigarette butt in to the street's dust, crossed over, and Tully murmured greeting. " 'Morning, Dave. Wonder if you got the same feeling I have."

"What's that, Jack?"

With a wave of a pudgy hand, Tully indicated the run of the street. "Same old street, same old town . . . yet both different. Because neither will ever see a good man again. Going to miss seeing Mel Rhodes moving about. Bad business, that."

Kerchival began building another smoke. "Jack, what's gone wrong with this damned range, anyhow?"

"Men," answered Tully briefly. "Nothing wrong in this world except men. Cross-grained streak in the brutes that makes them spoil things. Ain't never satisfied unless they're walking on the other fellow's neck. Got to prove that they're big, or something. I sit here and watch 'em come and go and try and figure out what makes 'em tick. So far I ain't found no good answer."

"Living can get complicated, Jack," said Kerchival dryly.

"Only if you want to make it so. A little food, a place to sleep, and time to sit and soak up the sun's goodness. Life can be as simple as that."

"That sun can get hot," Kerchival murmured.

"Never too hot for me," declared Tully. "I mind a time in the old cavalry days. We were trailing a bunch of renegade Nez Per-cés under Chief Joseph. Made suckers of us, Chief Joseph did. Led us into some high, open country where a blizzard hit us. Three days and nights that blizzard pounded us. Men froze to death trying to hold a sentry beat. I thought sure I was going to. Anyhow, those days and nights left a chill in me that a hundred years of hot sun won't ever thaw out. Some men need a jolt of whiskey to get 'em moving in the morning. Me, I'll take the sun."

Kerchival went over to Bus Spurgeon's after his horse. Bus

was moving sluggishly about his stable chores, bleary-eyed and dull from a sleepless night. He brought out Kerchival's horse, and Kerchival saddled it. Then he headed out of town, taking the Mount Cherokee slope trail. He kept well below Lazy Y headquarters, headed east across Kingfisher Creek, and climbed until he picked up the War Hatchet trail. Along this he lifted his horse to a quick jog.

It was a familiar trail, this one. He had ridden it before many times, and in those days the headquarters that lay at the end of it was home. But no longer.

Strange how far away that time seemed to be. Just a few short days when measured by simple run of time. But in terms of understanding, opinion, and purpose the gap was tremendous, far too wide ever to be bridged again. So much had happened in those few days to drive the iron of disillusionment deeply into a man, to light the fires of a still, cold fury, and to set a man's feet on a trail almost sure to know the haze and reek of gunsmoke.

It was not in Dave Kerchival's make-up to rant and rave and go noisy. He was the sort to go quietly under the lash, of anger or grief, and be more dangerous because of that. The frost and darkened, smoky look in his eyes were settled things now. His face was beaten into older lines and seemed all angles and flat, taut planes. He carried his shoulders in a forward, combative jut, and his hands and arms were restless with caged feeling. Once, this man had known a considerable capacity for whimsy and tolerant humor, but none of this was in him now.

War Hatchet headquarters seemed quiet, peaceful enough. But when Kerchival pulled up and dismounted, the door of the ranch office opened and Abel Hendron stepped out. They matched brittle stares as Kerchival moved up to face him. In Hendron he saw change.

Bleak hatred and animosity were there for him, which Kerchival expected. But there was more than that. There was a raggedness of expression, as though things long held deeply hidden and in abeyance to the will of this man had now surged to the surface and were breaking through, a weakening in that austere self-control.

Abel Hendron spoke, his voice rasping, harsh. "I believe I told you, when you left these premises, never to return."

Kerchival answered bluntly. "I'm here. Because I decided that it might be worth one more try to keep the cover from blowing off this range completely. You can help in that, if you want to."

"Finding the going rough, are you?" There was acid mockery in Abel Hendron's tone.

"Yeah," said Kerchival. "Rough and dirty. And likely to get worse. I'd a lot rather see it otherwise. Interested in calling quits?"

Abel Hendron laughed, a hard and mirthless sound. "You amuse me, Kerchival. You really do. After all the big talk you're whining now over lost marbles. You fool! Get off my land!"

Kerchival looked him up and down. "I was afraid it would be this way," he murmured quietly. "You miss the point entirely. So now you can have it in your teeth. I gave you a chance, Hendron . . . which is more than you deserve, I guess. Now I'll tell you how it will be. What you and the Ballards have started, I intend to finish. From where I stand now, it won't be a pretty finish. But then, you've written the rules, and now you'll have to play by them. There are going to be dead men along the trail. You've had your innings there. First Bill Yeager. Now Mel Rhodes. Maybe the written law will never be able to straighten out those two murky trails. But there is another law that came into being a long time ago. An eye for an eye. Remember?"

"You threaten me with things I do not understand," said Hendron. "What is this talk about Mel Rhodes?"

Kerchival laid his glance, hard and intent, on this man, trying to get behind the mask. Was Hendron's ignorance of Mel Rhodes's death feigned or real?

"Last night in his office," said Kerchival, "Mel Rhodes was stabbed to death. His safe was looted. Bill Yeager's will, which Mel was holding for me, was stolen. This morning, early, the Ballards and some others moved in on Lazy Y headquarters, ran Perk O'Dair and Chick Roland off, and took possession. You wouldn't try and tell me that this is all news to you, Hendron?"

Was that a glint of mocking triumph that flickered ever so briefly in Abel Hendron's masking brown eyes. He couldn't be sure, for it was so swiftly gone. Hendron shrugged.

"I knew of the Ballards moving in on Lazy Y," he admitted. "On my advice and suggestion. All this talk of a will has never fooled me, Kerchival. Where is such a will? I haven't seen it. Who *has* seen it? A few may have claimed to, just to further their own ends. I recognize nothing I can't see. And if you figure you can move in and take over Lazy Y, then others have the same right. I'm waiting for you to leave here, Kerchival. I'm warning you to, for the last time."

Now, Kerchival saw, there was no doubt of it. Abel Hendron was taunting, laughing at him. Kerchival's gray eyes went almost black. His words fell, grimly bitter.

"Count the cost, Hendron. It will be high. We'll deliver them to you, one by one. Across their saddles. Your precious nephews . . . the Ballards. You've run your little world to suit just yourself for so long you've developed a feeling that's gotten away from you. While you held your high and mighty ways to the limits of War Hatchet, nobody gave a damn. It just gave other men something to laugh at. But now you're trying to move into wider territory, where the cost will be high and the going rough. Always remember . . . you've asked for it."

Kerchival turned away, stepped into his saddle. Thin and dry as the whisper of a snake's rattles, Abel Hendron said: "I called you a fool. I call you that again. You had your warning. You had your chance. Now. . . ." He turned and called sharply: "Shugrue!"

A man eased into view past the corner of the ranch house. He was squat, thick-bodied, and he walked with clumping heaviness, planting his feet widely apart. His head was heavy, set close to his shoulders on a thick neck. His features were neutral because they carried no pattern or index of personality other than a heavy, unimaginative animalism. Here was the brute, cruel—starkly so. He carried two guns, low-swung, butts flaring and ready to thick, dangling hands.

Kerchival brought his horse around, stared past its ears at this man, Shugrue. Kerchival laughed mirthlessly. "Where did you drag that from, Hendron? Your tastes run pretty low these days. How much are you paying him for his guns?"

Kerchival knew that in Shugrue he was looking at a bought killer. He'd never seen the man before, but the fellow carried the signs of his feral profession as plainly as though he were branded with a skull and crossbones. Feeling crawled up Kerchival's spine, settled behind his eyes, with nerve ends singing with a fine, high tension that filled him with brittle alertness.

Abel Hendron spoke to Shugrue. "This man was warned never to put foot on my land again, under penalty. He must have thought I was bluffing, when he should have known that I never bluff. Well . . . ?"

Dave Kerchival said, half softly: "You want him dead, Hendron . . . right at your doorstep? That is the way it will be if you sic him on me. Just how small can you get, Hendron?"

Speaking, Dave Kerchival was working for a little more time, just a second or two. For he realized beyond all doubt that here was a showdown. He'd been working on the belief that somewhere in Abel Hendron there must be some shred of fairness, of human feeling. Apparently he'd been mistaken. The man was past all that now.

Kerchival had his reins in his left hand; his right lay along his thigh, just ahead of his holstered gun. And his glance was fixed on Shugrue, reading the resolve building up in the fellow's muddy eyes.

"Shugrue!" snapped Abel Hendron again. It was a command, stark and final.

Dave Kerchival saw the gunman's lips pinch down and knew that this was it. So Kerchival drove his spurs into his mount's flanks, lifting the startled horse forward in a long, lunging leap, straight at Shugrue.

Shugrue was going for his guns. This was what he'd been hired for, and Abel Hendron had given him his orders. He began his draw with a sort of stolid, unhurried speed, which could be the more deadly because of its measured certainty. But in the split-second interval between thought of purpose and the physical completion of it, Dave Kerchival was no longer a motionless target, up there on his horse. Now horse and man were blazing right in on the gunman, driving right at him. It shocked Shugrue with its unexpectedness, made him falter ever so slightly.

Things had been piling up in Dave Kerchival. Last night the sight of Mel Rhodes sprawled lifelessly on his office floor. This morning the fact that the Ballards had taken over at Lazy Y. And now Abel Hendron—cold, unbending, ungiving—ordering his death like some hardened, emotionless executioner. An inner explosiveness beat wildly in Kerchival. He was drawing at the first forward move of his horse.

Flame from Shugrue's guns bloomed palely and the hard report of them beat in Kerchival's ears. A wisp of his horse's mane seemed to leap and drift as though a blast of high wind had caught it. The horse reared and whirled as Shugrue's guns blasted a second time. Dave Kerchival felt his shirt tug and lift across the small of his back. Then he put his first shot in Shugrue's chest.

The shock of it seemed to beat the gunman back, to lift and hold him on his toes, while a vast and stricken wonder rolled up into his eyes. The wound was mortal, but life lay deep and stolid in Al Shugrue, and he was still dangerous as his guns began to chop down for a third try. Kerchival got there first, his second bullet placed not four inches from the first. This slug seemed to break up all reflex and co-ordination in Shugrue, who now swung half around, tottering. He walked right into the side of the ranch house, reeled away, and fell over backward.

Dave Kerchival brought his wheeling, lunging horse around, and dropped his gun across his body so that the reeking muzzle was looking Abel Hendron squarely in the eye.

"You see, Hendron? Number one. There'll be more!"

Kerchival set back on the reins, backing his horse away. The gunshots had sent hard, ripping echoes tumbling back and forth among the ranch buildings, giving plenty of alarm to anyone about the place. But no one showed.

Kerchival spun his horse and lifted it into a run. Abel Hendron, erect and frozen of face, stood there on his office steps, staring at the tumbled heap that was Al Shugrue, hired gunman.

CHAPTER NINE

Dave Kerchival rode straight back to town. His mood was a shadowy, bitter one. That shoot-out had been thrust upon him. He knew no exultation over winning it. It had been like shooting down a surly dog. But Abel Hendron had ordered it, had called Shugrue in to his death, though that was not the way Hendron had planned it. It was proof of how deeply Abel Hendron had committed himself to a ruthless drive for complete mastery of the Mount Cherokee plateau range, slope and top, and that he'd burned all his bridges behind him. There could be no pause now, no arbitration or peace, until Hendron was whipped, or until he fulfilled his lust for empire. People were going to be hurt, among them Lear Hendron. No matter how this thing came out, that girl was going to be hurt. Kerchival knew a twisting regret over this realization.

The only reason he'd made a final appeal to Abel Hendron for a peaceful settling of this thing was because of Lear. For, with things going the way they were, it was entirely possible that he would be faced with the necessity of throwing a gun on Abel Hendron. And if this should happen, then there would be a gulf between Lear and himself that nothing could ever bridge. No matter how fully justified he might be in such an act, the result would be the same. It would alienate the girl completely and forever.

In town Kerchival tied his horse in front of Sam Liederman's store, went in, found a shadowy corner, and perched on a nail keg, there to smoke and think and await the return of Dusty Elliot, Perk O'Dair, and Chick Roland.

In a state of subdued apathy Sam Liederman moved about his store and waited on occasional trade and did other routine chores. The rotund little storekeeper had been genuinely fond of Mel Rhodes, and he was sick and stunned over the latter's savage death. Once he came over to Kerchival and made harsh demand: "Why do you sit there? Why don't you do somethin'? He was your friend, too. It is because of business he was handlin' for you that he's dead. Why don't you do something?"

Kerchival answered with an almost gentle tolerance. He understood how Sam felt. The storekeeper was just a kindly little man, now mixed up and sadly hurt, desirous of hitting out at something, but not knowing exactly what.

"Can't rush a thing like this, Sam," said Kerchival quietly. "We've got to know some facts before we can move. So far, we don't. Keep your shirt on. Plenty is going to be done, because this thing has just started."

Sam got hold of himself, dropped a hand on Kerchival's shoulder. "I know, Dave," he mumbled. "Sorry. I'm just all jangled to pieces."

It was pushing midday when hoofs came rattling into town. Kerchival, cocking an alert ear, identified the sound as two horses. He went to the store door and Perk O'Dair and Chick Roland, spying him, swung their sweating ponies to the rail. Kerchival went over to them.

"Well?"

"Only sign of life we could make out around Ballard headquarters was that half-breed cook of theirs," reported Perk. "And no horses left in the cavvy corral."

"Good enough," said Kerchival. "Let's go over to the A-1 and eat."

Chick, noting the bleakness in Kerchival's eyes, said: "You

look fifty degrees tougher now than when we left, Dave. You went somewhere and bumped into something. Perk and me would like to know."

Kerchival considered a moment, then told them. "I went out to War Hatchet. Aimed to try one more appeal to Abel Hendron to slow up before this thing blew wide open. It didn't work. He practically admitted that having the Ballards move in on Lazy Y was his idea. Never saw Hendron looking so wild and ragged around the edges. Something he's been covering up for a long time has begun to break through in the man, and it's not good to look at. Maybe I needled him a little more than was necessary, but, when I was set to leave, he called up a hired gunfighter he'd picked up somewhere. Called the fellow Shugrue."

Kerchival paused, the somberness in his look and tone deepening.

"You mean," demanded Perk O'Dair, "that Hendron sicced a gunfighter on you, then and there?"

"That's right. I guess he figured it was a prime chance to move me out of the picture, once and for all."

"But it didn't work!" Perk exclaimed. "You're here, and all in one piece as far as I can see. What happened, Dave?"

Kerchival shrugged. "Shugrue started to draw. I killed him."

The very bluntness of the statement held Perk and Chick still and considerably awed. They stared at Kerchival, and then stared away. Chick spoke finally, a hardness molding his words: "Abel Hendron tried to do that to you? When you'd worked for him for five years, taken care of his interests as though they were your own, and never did him a wrong in your life? Yet he was ready to throw a gunfighter at you and have you smoked down . . . Dave, the man's crazy."

"Crazy, nothin'!" exploded Perk. "Meaner than hell, that's what. I don't hold with this way of excusin' a man's orneriness by sayin' he's crazy. There's always been a vicious streak in Abel

Hendron, but he never had need of showin' too much of it while things were rollin' to suit him. But when things begin to pile up ahead of him, then the mean begins to show. Lots of *hombres* are that way. Dave, had I been in your boots, after I'd downed that Shugrue feller, I think I'd have throwed down on Hendron himself."

"No, Perk," differed Kerchival quietly, "I don't think you would."

Perk squirmed restlessly. "You're right," he admitted gruffly. "I wouldn't have. I'd have been thinking of Lear Hendron."

"Exactly," murmured Kerchival.

They ate in silence. Kerchival was vaguely amazed that he had any appetite for food. This right hand of his, sinewy and brown, that held his knife—just a few short hours before, it had dealt death to a man. Now it was cutting steak to feed a demanding stomach. *Where,* he thought sardonically, *were all the fine theories of man's civilized state now? The veneer was parchment-thin. Scratch through it and there lay the dark and fierce breath of the jungle. Kill or be killed. The survival of the fit—all that sort of thing. Trite, but fundamentally true. The primitive forces of life were more powerful than all the fine theories ever concocted. . . .*

They had just finished their meal when Dusty Elliot and Brace Shotwell came clanking in. "Sam Liederman said you were over here," reported Dusty briefly. "Brace and Joe Kirby are anxious to know your plans, Dave."

"I let you down, Brace," said Kerchival. "I told you I'd hang onto Lazy Y, and then didn't make good."

Brace Shotwell cut a hand across in front of him in a discarding gesture. "Water under the bridge, Dave. Not your fault. Not anybody's fault. Dusty told me how it happened. Same thing could have happened to anybody. Question is . . . where do we go from here?"

"Out to Ballard headquarters . . . first. When you want to run rats off the premises, it's always a good move to clean out the nest. After that, we make a little call at Lazy Y headquarters."

Brace Shotwell met Kerchival's glance, recognized the hard resolve in Kerchival's eyes, then nodded. "That's the stuff. Carry it to them." He nodded again. "Joe and the other boys will like this."

"Better get your crowd in here to feed," said Kerchival. "From here on in it could be a long time between meals."

Half an hour later they left town. Shotwell and Kirby had brought along a round dozen men, hard-bitten plains riders, ready for anything. They angled up the slope range, keeping a steady drift to the west. They moved out of the clear area and into the first scattered timber, riding fast.

The sun thrust golden lances through the timber, laying a sharp criss-cross of light and shadow. The air was warm and full of the pleasant bite of resin. Brooding silence opened, let them through with the muffled thump of hoofs and the creak of saddle gear, then closed behind them and took over again.

Miles along, up close to the rim, they crossed the moist, fern-lined headwaters of Warm Creek, and after that moved with increasing wariness while Dusty and Perk and Chick scouted ahead. They circled completely past the Ballard headquarters, then came in on the place from the west.

It lay in a little basin between two rolls of timbered slope. A couple of cabins, a cook shack, corrals, and feed sheds. Kerchival called a halt just inside the edge of the timber and watched the place for a little time. A figure appeared in the door of the cook shack, tossed a pan of dishwater out, then disappeared again. It was as Perk and Chick had reported. Nobody on hand but the cook. Kerchival shook his reins.

"All right," he said. "Let's go on in!"

They moved out into the clearing, spread out and wary, just

in case. They were within fifty yards when the cook, warned by the mutter of hoofs, came to the doorway of the cook shack and stood, staring. A moment later he would have ducked in, but Kerchival's harsh order—"Stay right there!"—held him in the open.

The cook was a half-breed, sullen, frowsy, untidy, and frankly scared. "Stand clear and you won't get hurt," Kerchival told him. "Try anything and it'll be just too bad."

"What's the idee?" mumbled the cook. "What d'you want?"

"Why," drawled Kerchival, "it's just a little matter of possession. The Ballards took over my place, and I'm taking over theirs. And, having taken over, I don't like the looks of the layout. It's a blot on the fair face of the world. So. . . ."

While speaking, Dave Kerchival was unstrapping his reata from his saddle fork. He shook out a small loop. Now his voice crackled.

"Stand aside, I said!"

The cook scuttled into the clear. Kerchival rode up to one of the cabins, flipped his reata loop over a jutting eave's log end, threw a dally on his saddle horn, and moved his horse into the pull. Dusty Elliot gave his usual exclamation.

"Hah! I get it. Come on, Perk, Chick!"

Perk and Chick put their ropes on the same log end, while Dusty looped another at the cabin's corner. Brace Shotwell and Joe Kirby and their riders moved in, adding their ropes here and there. With bunched haunches and straining tendons, the horses began putting their weight into the pull. Saddle girths and latigos creaked, ropes stretched stingingly tight.

Cabin logs squeaked protest but began to give. Dust exploded in little gusts from tortured crevices, and joists groaned under the build up of destroying power. Split shakes on the roof buckled and cracked. And then, from every angle at once, it seemed, the cabin came apart, walls toppling, roof caving in with a crash. Within one short minute what had been a reasonably sound, snug cabin was just a tumbled, twisted tangle of logs, of splintered rafters and shakes, a mess of débris covering and burying whatever the cabin had held.

Dave Kerchival slacked his rope, freed the loop. "Now for the next," he said remorselessly.

Given the same treatment, the second cabin went down. The cook shack followed. Then feed sheds and corrals. The clearing resounded with the crashing and splintering. When it was all done, Kerchival surveyed the result with a critical eye while he coiled his rope.

"They'll know damned little satisfaction with that mess when they see it again," he said. Then he added ominously: "If they ever do!"

He rode over to the cook, who stood dazed and sullen. "This," Kerchival told him, "ought to convince you of something or other. Maybe that Ballard men are going to be highly unpopular in these parts from now on. Use your own judgment, friend, but I'd suggest a change of scenery."

Kerchival turned his horse's head to the east. "Now for the other chore," he ordered.

The half-breed cook watched them go, watched until the timber had swallowed them. Then he looked over at the tangled mess that had once been a headquarters, and gave vent to a frenzy of wild cursing. This out of his system, he went over to the pile of rubbish that had once been a cook shack, and began digging around in the débris. He came up eventually with a couple of blankets and a greasy old war bag. He made a rough pack out of these and headed upslope toward the rim.

It was a long trip across Mount Cherokee for a man on foot, but it was a good way out of the country.

CHAPTER TEN

At Abel Hendron's War Hatchet headquarters a gray and wrenching bitterness held everyone and everything. It was as though something that had always been a unit was now splitting and drawing apart into several pieces, leaving a vacuum of strain and uneasiness.

When the rolling smash of gun echoes had stilled, and when Dave Kerchival had ridden away, Abel Hendron had stood very still for a long time, staring at the huddled figure of Al Shugrue, almost as gross and formidable in death as he had been in life.

The savage abruptness with which the gunfighter had died before Dave Kerchival's gun was a shock that left Hendron chilled and dazed. For this man Shugrue had come to him, recommended as being almost without parallel when it came to handling a deadly gun. Yet, in the ultimate test, Dave Kerchival had outthought, outmaneuvered, and outshot him. Shugrue had died. Kerchival had ridden away, unhurt. Staring at that lifeless figure, Hendron searched for an answer he couldn't find.

Hendron tore his eyes from the dead figure, swung his glance to where Kerchival had disappeared along the out trail. Underneath Hendron's cold remoteness the fires seethed and raged, draining the blood from his face. But there was more than thwarted rage working. Far back, pushing up from the man's innate but carefully hidden caution, writhed a thread of uneasiness, the beginnings of fear.

Had he made the cardinal mistake of underestimating the

capacity of Dave Kerchival? That was all it took, Abel Hendron knew, to wreck the most carefully conceived dream of range conquest—just to guess completely wrong on one major factor.

He grappled with the unease of this thought, pushed it back, smothered it with the weight of his own limitless ego. He turned and went into the house, passing through his office and on into the spacious living room beyond. In here was Lear Hendron and her brother Virg.

Lear stood by the center table, her hands pressing down upon it. Her face was dead white, her eyes big and dark and full of a dreadful, nameless revulsion. She looked at her father as though he were a complete stranger she was seeing from a great distance. That look stung Abel Hendron, aroused a roughness in him. He knew exactly what she was thinking about and he spoke harshly.

"When Kerchival first showed, riding in, I told you to go to your room," he said harshly. "Why didn't you obey?"

She spoke, not answering him, but as though voicing her thoughts aloud: "It's no use. I can't go on making lying excuses to myself any longer. Maybe to others, but not to myself."

"What are you talking about?" rapped Abel Hendron. "What's this rubbish about lying excuses?"

She spoke directly to him now. "Lying excuses for the things you do and would do. I've been doing that for so long. Now I never will again."

This did things to the Hendron pride. The idea of there being a necessity for making lying excuses for the acts of any Hendron—Abel Hendron told his daughter as much, blazing.

She shook her head wearily. "That does no good. I'm sick of the hypocrisy of it. Just now I heard . . . and I saw. I saw Dave Kerchival ride in here and I heard him try and talk fairness and sense and reason with you. In answer you mocked and jeered at him. And at the same time you were scheming . . . slyly, treacherously . . . that he shouldn't ride away from here alive. You had that . . . that Shugrue hidden out and waiting only for your word. And you gave that word. So . . . there will be no more excuses. I will no longer live under this roof!"

Lear turned to leave the room. Her father caught her by the arm, jerked her around. Her expression did not change. She just looked at him and looked at him and looked at him. Abel Hendron tried to meet that look, to beat it down. He ground his small white teeth in anger over his inability to do so. This girl, this slim daughter of his, had abruptly become as remote from him and his authority and influence as the most distant star from the earth. His grip on her arm loosened and she pushed his hand away. She walked out, her shoulders very straight.

Virg Hendron stirred uneasily. "You talk of pride," he muttered. "You just saw some that was really honest. For the first time the word has a real meaning to me."

Abel Hendron whirled on his son, letting go his bottled-up wrath. "Why didn't you come outside with me as I ordered, when Kerchival showed? Or wasn't your nerve up to it?"

Virg's lips twisted. "What kind of nerve are you talking about? The kind that has a professional gunfighter laying out around a corner, waiting to work on a man who doesn't know he's there? If that's what you call nerve, then I don't want any part of it. I don't blame Lear for finally gagging and calling it quits. That was about as low a deal as could be pulled off the bottom of a dirty deck."

Abel Hendron squared away in front of his son, half lifted a hand as though to strike him across the mouth.

Virg stood up, held his ground. "That," he warned bluntly, "would be an awful bad mistake. Now, I'd have gone out with you if I'd had any idea of what was in the wind, which was that you were intending to throw Shugrue at Kerchival. Yeah, I'd have gone out and yelled a warning to Kerchival. Now if that doesn't make sense to you, it's because it doesn't make much to me, either. I'm not trying to play noble. I'm not in Lear's class. Up to now she's been loyal because she's been a good daughter to you. Me, I've been loyal because it was easier that way, an easier ride than thinking and acting for myself. I guess I'll still string along. But somehow I know I'd sure have warned Dave Kerchival, and I'm glad of that."

"You and your sister are a pair of young fools," charged Abel Hendron in cold anger. "What do you think I've been building for? Why do you think I go on building? For myself? No! For you . . . for the pair of you. For your future and the future of the Hendron name. You're blind if you can't see that."

Virg looked at his father with the keenest discernment he had ever known. He shook his head. "I'm not so sure of that. That those are your true reasons, I mean. And if they are, they're still wrong. Take me, for instance. Even I'm beginning to understand that there's more to life than just acres of range and cows to graze those acres. There's the way a man goes about getting those things. If they don't come clean, then they don't mean anything. I'd rather have less of them and more of friends . . . more of the liking and respect of good men. Have we got any such friends? I can't name any. All we've got are the Ballards."

There was a twist of contempt in Virg's final words and Abel Hendron's temper began to flare again.

"They're your cousins and faithful to the family welfare. They took possession of Lazy Y and are keeping possession of it. What are you doing?"

"Beginning to really think for the first time in my life," retorted Virg. "And, because of that, staying out of an affair that's starting to smell to high heaven. If you want the Ballards, you can have 'em. I'm beginning to see them just like Lear does."

Virg started to leave, but Abel Hendron snapped: "I'll need help getting Shugrue out of sight."

"It'll take a horse to move that clod," said Virg. "Or a wheelbarrow."

"Get the wheelbarrow," ordered his father.

"All right. But only because I don't want Shugrue lying there for Lear to see."

Virg got the wheelbarrow and a blanket and, with his father's help, performed the grisly chore of getting a dead man out of sight.

In the house Lear Hendron moved about her room, dry-eyed and still of face. As far back as she could remember, this room had been a major part of her world, her haven and sanctuary. Now she was making ready to leave it, forever and for good reason, she told herself. She began packing an old gripsack.

Her packing done, she set herself to wait her chance to leave. She wanted to go without further words or argument. If she tried to leave in front of her father, it would only mean another scene. Even though she had told her father flatly that she would no longer live under his roof, she doubted that he felt she really meant it. It was so much a part of his make-up never to admit, even to himself, that anything he was against, or which he did not want to take place, would ever occur. That children of his would ever, of their own volition, leave the shelter of his roof for the reason that they could no longer stand to remain under it was something Abel Hendron's vanity and ego would simply never admit.

It was a cold and dreadful thing, that vanity, that ego. It demanded so much. It was something that had to be fed and catered to at all times. It made its own rules, its own laws. It made wrong right and black white. It was as false as all untruth, but as tenacious as death. And this day Lear Hendron could take no more of it. She crouched by the window of her room, waiting for the hours to pass and for her chance to leave this house.

CHAPTER ELEVEN

At the foot of a sugar pine a few yards distant from the cabin door at Lazy Y headquarters, a rider lounged. Leaning against the tree beside him was a rifle. The rider smoked and yawned and cursed his luck at having to stand guard in this broad light of day while the luckier of his fellows either slept or sat in on the poker game going on in the cabin. As far as he was concerned, this rider saw no sense at all in having a daylight guard. At night things might be different; then men could come sneaking in from the timber. But anyone who tried that sort of thing at this time of day would be crazy. They'd be cut to ribbons before they got anywhere near the cabin.

Gard Ballard appeared at the cabin door. "All quiet, Reeder?"

"Hell, yes," growled Reeder. "What do you expect? Nobody would be fool enough to try and rush this place in broad daylight. Ain't a soul within miles except our own crowd."

So spoke the guard, and immediately knew he was completely wrong. For, with a wicked *phflut* something struck the ground not a yard in front of him, showering him with pine needles and dirt, then whimpering away in buzzing ricochet. From a point out at the edge of the little bench land, a rifle sent hard echoes rocketing. Reeder, the guard, moved faster than ever before in his life. He caught up his rifle and ran, all in one jump. He dived in at the cabin door past Gard Ballard like a scared ground hog into its burrow.

Out where that rifle had crashed its challenge, Dusty Elliot swung the lever of his Winchester, pumping in a fresh shell. Crouched beside him, Dave Kerchival said: "That's their warning. They know we're here. Now to see if there's just a thin ounce of common sense left in them."

"There ain't," declared Dusty. "They never did have any sense, them Ballards, so how can they have any now? You'll make a mistake if you offer 'em any kind of break at all."

"You're probably completely right," Kerchival admitted. "Yet I've got to do it. You cover me. But no more shooting unless they really ask for it."

"You," charged Dusty desperately, "are a darn' fool if you go tryin' to crawl up close enough for them to hear you. You'll get picked off, sure. I'd sooner trust a blind rattlesnake than any one of them guys."

"We'll see," said Kerchival. "We've got to remember, Dusty, that when they had Perk and Chick dead to rights, they let the two kids ride out with whole skins. We've got to offer them the same break. Here goes."

He was gone before Dusty could argue any further. He moved straight in on the cabin, slipping from the shelter of one tree to another. Swearing steadily to himself, Dusty shifted his position to get a little better over-all view of the headquarters and watched with straining eyes and ready rifle.

Dave Kerchival, working in through the sugar pines, felt in his heart that Dusty Elliot was probably right on all counts. Talking to the Ballards, trying to get them to move off Lazy Y without making a fight of it, would probably get him nowhere. But it was something he had to try, else the ghosts of dead men would ride him forever. At first it was not difficult to keep hidden, for here the timber was fairly thick and, moving at a crouch, a man could slip from the protection of one massive bole to another, always going ahead. But as he drew within hailing distance of the cabin, the timber thinned and now there were definite gaps to cross, intervals in which a man might be picked off by some alert rifleman in the cabin.

There was a window on this side of the cabin, and Kerchival, pausing behind a friendly trunk to study it, saw the sun strike up a bright shine on worn steel. A man was there—a man with a gun. Kerchival measured the distance to a final tree, gathered himself, and darted across. That rifle at the window whipped down, but no report came, for Kerchival was a stride to the good and had gained his shelter before the rifleman could get his sights lined up.

Back at his point of watchfulness, Dusty Elliot saw that rifle at the window and he drew a bead on the orifice, holding just above the sill, and mumbling to himself: "If Dave tries to get any closer, that guy at the window will try and pot him, sure. So I'll have to get there first."

Dusty cuddled the stock of his rifle tightly against his cheek, his finger taut and ready on the trigger.

But Dave Kerchival did not try to get any closer. From here he could say all he had to. He cupped his hands about his mouth and sent the call echoing.

"Hey, Ballard . . . Gard Ballard! This is Kerchival! Got something to tell you!"

For a moment or two there was no answer. Then Gard Ballard sent his harsh return: "Ain't a thing you can tell us, Kerchival. We're here and here we stay. That's final!"

"Better think on it," warned Kerchival. "I ain't alone. I've got plenty men backing my hand. You can ride away from here now and keep your skins whole. You've got my word on that. But if you're set to make a fight of it, then it's going to be rough. This is for keeps! You've got five minutes to make up your mind."

"Don't need five minutes . . . don't need one minute!" came Gard Ballard's taunting shout. "You think you can root us out of here, let's see you try."

The man at the window with the rifle now dropped his weapon in line and levered three quick shots. One slug thudded solidly into the tree in front of Kerchival. The other two, skimming the edges of things, ripped chunks of bark and slivers off the tree and sent them buzzing.

Now his yell came, hoarse and heavy. "Try and get away from that tree! You won't last two jumps. We'll see who's got who bottled up. You're pocketed, trapped like a 'coon. Go ahead. Make your try!"

Dave Kerchival, looking around, saw that there was plenty of uncomfortable truth in this—too much. Moving in before they had him fully located was one thing. Backing away now that they were alert and waiting was something else again. Dusty had been right.

Kerchival twisted his head, gauging distance. Fifteen yards would do it. Once he got that far he could make it the rest of the way without too much risk. But those first fifteen yards were long ones and grisly with danger. Yet he couldn't stay here. Risk or no risk, he wasn't going to stay crouched behind this tree for the rest of the day while the Ballards and their crowd gave him the horselaugh.

"Dusty," he muttered, "I hope you're watching. Here goes."

Kerchival slid his six-shooter past the side of the tree, emptied it in a flashing roll of shots at that threatening window. Then he whirled and ran.

The rifle at the window slithered snakily, settled into line. And that was when the faithful, watching Dusty, farther back in the timber, pressed the trigger of his rifle. Dusty didn't have much to shoot at. Just a vague suggestion of a man's head and shoulder, muffled by the gloom of the cabin's inner shadow.

Dusty's bullet told with a thud, and the shadowy target he had pulled on sagged swiftly from sight. The threatening rifle teetered across the window sill for a moment, then tipped and fell outside the cabin. From inside came a hoarse, hard yell of bitter anger. And all of these things told a grim story that made Chick Roland, crouched a little behind Dusty, give a queer sound in his throat.

Dusty, levering in another shell and still intent on that window, said briefly: "This ain't checkers we're playin', kid."

Now from all sides the snarl of rifle fire lifted, and slugs smashed through windows and door or thudded into cabin walls. This burst of firing was brief, however, for Dave Kerchival had given his men their orders when he first sent them out to make the surround.

"Just enough lead to let them know we're watching on all sides," was how Kerchival had put it for Brace Shotwell and Joe Kirby.

And while the brief burst of fire had undoubtedly done this, it had, along with Dusty's deadly shot, served another purpose. It had enabled Dave Kerchival to get safely back into the heavier timber. Now, panting, he dropped in beside Dusty.

"Owe you one for that, cowboy. I was praying you were set and ready. You were!"

Strained silence settled down. A Douglas squirrel let out one chattering, frightened bark from the lofty top of a pine, then went still. Dusty spoke, while plugging a couple of fresh shells through the loading gate of his rifle.

"Right now they're beginnin' to sweat. Figured they were real smart, they did. They'd run the kids off and then, with them in possession, and figurin' they only had us four to worry about, they calculated they had us damn' well licked. Now they know different. Now they're in a jackpot. I'll bet there's some tall old cussin' and name-callin' goin' on in that cabin."

Kerchival built a cigarette. "They've got something to think about, all right. Now they'll probably lay quiet until dark. Then they may try something. Either a break for a mass getaway, or

113

maybe slip one man out to go for help. Most likely the last."

"Where'd he go for help?" demanded Dusty.

"War Hatchet, of course."

"Think they'd get it?"

"Sure they would. Hendron is in this just as deep as they are . . . deeper, really. He's staked more on this game, so has more to lose."

"Maybe so," said Dusty. "But who's Hendron got to send? When you and me and Perk and Chick left him, he lost his crew. All he's got left is old Deaf Blair, himself, and Virg. And Deaf Blair sure ain't goin' to pick up a gun for Abel Hendron to use on his former bunkies. Old Deaf just ain't that kind of *hombre*."

"You're forgetting that fellow Shugrue, Dusty," said Kerchival dryly. "I'm not. I don't think I ever will. Hendron's been replacing us, cowboy. If he could bring in the likes of Shugrue, he could bring in more of the same stripe. Like the four strangers with the Ballards."

"Guess you're right," Dusty admitted. "Well, anyhow, at the present readin' they're shy a couple of their bully boys. You got Shugrue and I was dead on that jigger in the window. And now I'm bettin' that some of those hired hands in yonder are beginnin' to wonder if they aren't sitting in a pretty thin deal."

Chick Roland had moved up beside them. Chick looked a trifle tight around the eyes and lips. Kerchival saw that Chick needed something else to think about than the man who had bulked at the cabin window.

"Got a chore for you, kid. Skin out for town. Borrow a pack bronco from Bus Spurgeon and load it with grub at Sam Liederman's. We've got a flock of men to feed here, and this thing could drag on for a couple of days. One thing is sure. It will go on until we've run that crowd out of the cabin."

Chick nodded and went away, crouched and cautious. Dusty

spoke softly: "Chick and Perk are pretty stout kids, but, same as with anybody else, first time around, the sniff of gunsmoke is kinda rough. But I'll bet a leg on either of 'em, when the last chip is down." Dusty leaned his rifle against a tree, reached for his smoking. "Goin' to be some slow hours between now and sundown."

"Don't let them lull you to sleep," cautioned Kerchival. "I'm going to make the rounds and tell the boys to sit tight and wait this thing out. After which, I think I'll take a little scout out to the east. Just in case. I wouldn't want Hendron and a bunch to come prowling and catch us with our backs turned."

Kerchival found Brace Shotwell and the plains riders on the job and missing nothing. He told them the outcome of his attempt to reason with the Ballards.

"That's what they think now," growled the weather-beaten cattleman. "Wait'll they've been cooped up in there for a couple of days."

Kerchival went out to where all their horses were grouped under the guard of Perk O'Dair. From here the cabin was not visible. Perk had heard the shooting and was all a-squirm with curiosity and impatience.

"Hell of a chore to draw," he complained. "Nothin' to do but stand around an' chew my fingernails. I want to be up where the fun is goin' on, Dave."

"No fun, kid," said Kerchival bluntly. "There's a dead man in the cabin . . . now."

"Huh?" ejaculated Perk. "Oh! You mean a man. . . ."

"Yeah. A dead one. In the cabin."

"Um," Perk mumbled, and began building a smoke. "That rough, eh?"

"That rough." Kerchival led out his horse and stepped into the saddle.

He circled well back from Lazy Y headquarters and headed

for Kingfisher Creek. He crossed this and angled cautiously on to War Hatchet range. He kept to the cover of timber as much as possible, circling meadows, staying off ridge tops. He had no illusions as to his future status with Abel Hendron and War Hatchet. After the Shugrue affair Kerchival knew that he would be open game to Hendron, or any of his imported gun toughs, any time, anywhere.

Which did not worry him particularly. The iron of this affair was rampant in him now. None of it had been of his making. He had tried the words of peace and had been met with the smoke and lead of open war. So that was the way it would be now, until the final answer was written. Again his thoughts reached a lone regret—Lear Hendron.

Kerchival struck another spread of timber, rode through it, and was about to break into the clear beyond the far edge, when a vague stirring ran across his nerve ends, an alertness that came out of nowhere with all the startling shock of a glass of cold water in the face. He reined in, listening, twisting in his saddle, his glance reaching and testing the shadowy timber on all sides. Nothing moved or showed except a pair of pine siskins, fluttering about a branch tip near by.

Kerchival dismounted, slid his rifle free of the saddle boot, stole to the timber edge, and looked out and down across a small, cupped meadow. He went very still.

Two riders were in sight, less than two hundred yards distant. They sat their saddles, facing each other, talking. They were well beyond earshot, but close enough to be clearly identified. One was Abel Hendron. The other was Jack Tully.

Abel Hendron sat his saddle just as he walked, stiffly erect and unbending, precise and spare. Jack Tully, shorter, meatier, slouched, riding his weight on the near stirrup. How long they had been there, Kerchival had no idea. There was no chance to get close enough to hear what they were saying. All he could do was watch and wonder.

Abruptly a startling thing happened. Abel Hendron went for his gun. Jack Tully thereupon displayed talents with which no one, observing the manner in which he lounged and loafed about town, would ever have credited him. He moved like a striking snake, and his gun was out and covering Hendron before the latter got halfway there. Kerchival started to lift his rifle, unconsciously caught up by the threat that seemed about to explode. But Jack Tully did not shoot. Instead, he kneed his horse closer to Hendron, whose hands now lifted slowly to a level with his ears.

Jack Tully leaned over and, with his free hand, lifted Hendron's gun. He seemed to give an order, which he emphasized with a little wave of his ready weapon. Abel Hendron lowered his hands, caught up his reins, turned his horse, and rode east along the meadow.

Jack Tully watched him cover a hundred yards, then spun his own mount and sent it at a scudding run, sweeping up out of the meadow, then down and around the timber patch below Kerchival. Abel Hendron never looked back once. His horse climbed the low rim of the meadow to the east, dropped out of sight beyond.

The world was empty. Dave Kerchival blinked his eyes, wondering if this thing had really taken place, or if he was seeing things. What did it mean? What did it add up to? Where did Jack Tully fit into the picture of Abel Hendron's plans? Or did he? Why had Hendron tried to draw on Tully, and why hadn't Tully smoked him down for it? For that matter, since when had pudgy Jack Tully, whose favorite loafing place was the bench beside Sam Liederman's store door in town, started riding the hills and showing startling dexterity with a gun?

Questions hammered at Dave Kerchival's brain, but no single satisfactory answer came to any of them. He built a cigarette and smoked it to the last ash before going back to his horse. And then, although he pondered this strange meeting all the way back to Lazy Y headquarters, he had no semblance of a satisfactory answer to anything.

Dusty Elliot had nothing to report. "Everythin' quiet, Dave. Probably like you say. They're waitin' for dark before startin' somethin'."

CHAPTER TWELVE

Chick Roland came trailing in half an hour ahead of dusk. With him rode Joe Orchard. The deputy looked gray and tired and discouraged. He turned on Dave Kerchival almost harshly. "What goes on in this damn' country? I came in past the Ballard headquarters not too long ago. Not a building left standing. Looked like a cyclone had hit it. Now I come in here and there's guys with guns hid out behind every tree and blow down. Mebbe I don't count around here any more. Mebbe folks just aim to make their own law as they go along. You think so, mebbe?"

Kerchival shrugged. "You got a better answer, Joe? Nothing against you or the law, understand. But what would you have me and the other boys do . . . fold up and let Hendron and the Ballards run us out of the country?"

"Oh, hell!" growled Joe wearily. "You know it ain't that, Dave. It ain't anything you've done or are fixing to do, for that matter. In your boots I'd feel the same as you do. But I'm supposed to be the law and I'm supposed to call the turns. And so far I ain't been able to. I got two dead men on my mind that I'm supposed to find the killers of. Right now I ain't a single damn' inch closer to an answer than I was when I first started looking for one. I can guess plenty, but I can't prove a thing." He paused and scrubbed a hand across his eyes, then added: "Chick's been telling me about things. Told me about your trouble at War Hatchet this morning, with the Shugrue *hombre*. That was a pretty raw move by Abel Hendron."

"Yeah. And right here you're looking at another one, Joe," said Kerchival. "The Ballards ran Perk and Chick off Lazy Y at gun point. When you take over that way, that makes it forcible entry in big letters. Now it's our turn. We're going to run them out. If it takes a week, if it takes a month. They're going to get as good as they send."

"I got to make a try at heading this thing off before any more dead men get spread around," said Joe. "I'm going into that cabin for a talk."

"You show yourself and they'll smoke you down, Joe," protested Dusty Elliot. "Dave had the idea he could talk to them jiggers, too . . . and darn' near got shot realizin' he couldn't."

"Difference between Dave and me," grunted the deputy. He moved up ahead slightly, cupped his hands about his lips, and yelled: "This is Joe Orchard. I'm coming in for a talk. You hear me?"

The echoes of the deputy's call ran out. Then came the muffled answer. "Come on in, Orchard. But come alone!"

Joe Orchard straightened and walked straight for the cabin.

Dusty Elliot squirmed and swore. "They double-cross Joe. . . ."

"They won't," cut in Kerchival. "They wouldn't dare."

Through the blue dusk Joe Orchard plodded on to the cabin door, not a big man and one no longer young. But one whose middle name was courage. The cabin door swung back and he went in. Fifteen minutes later he emerged and came back at the same unhurried walk.

"They ain't happy in there at all," he reported. "They got a dead man in there, and the rest are pretty edgy. When I told 'em how many men you had spread around, I could sure see their ears droop. If you'll let 'em go peaceable, Dave, I think I can talk 'em into pulling out right now."

"They can go that way," agreed Kerchival. "But tell 'em not to try and come back."

Joe Orchard headed for the cabin again. Dusty Elliot said harshly: "I guess there wasn't much else we could do, Dave, but I'll never feel easy about things until them three Ballards are in hell with their throats cut. Somethin' tells me we're goin' to have to do all this over again. Make good dogs outta them, I mean."

"I'm still remembering they let Perk and Chick go," said Kerchival. "For that they've got to have their break."

Joe Orchard stood at the cabin door and talked. Then he stepped to one side. Two men came out, carrying a dead man between them. Four more followed, the last three being the Ballards—Gard, Spence, and Turk.

"Come on!" ordered Dave Kerchival.

He and Dusty moved in toward the cabin. Brace Shotwell and Joe Kirby and some of their men came in from other angles. They gathered in a grim circle about the discomfited Ballards and their men. One of the latter turned on Gard Ballard with a bitter curse. "Four, you said . . . or mebbe six at the outside, was what you told us, with two of them bein' those kids we run out this mornin'. Now look at 'em. Can't you count? We'd have raised hell, we would, tryin' to break through this crowd!"

"We're letting you go for one reason," said Dave Kerchival curtly. "Because you let Perk and Chick go this morning. But don't make the mistake of trying to come back here. Next time things will be really rough."

One of the strangers with the Ballards glanced at the dead man. "Plenty rough enough for me this trip," he said.

The Ballards were surly, saying nothing. The dead man was tied across a saddle. The rest, bringing their horses from the corrals, mounted and rode away into night's quickening gloom.

Brace Shotwell, standing at Dave Kerchival's shoulder, growled: "If things were reversed, I wonder would they have done as much by us, Dave? Sometimes I think being a reasonably decent sort of *hombre* is a fool's business and a handicap in getting along in the world."

Kerchival said: "Brace, how long before you flat-country cowmen can get your summering herds moving up Kingfisher?"

"A week, ten days at the outside. Why? Little early to start thinking about moving them up to the plateau, ain't it? Our lower range will carry all right for another month or six weeks."

"Be wise to make the drive a little early this year, I think. If I had that will, it'd be different. It would be a record of ownership they couldn't bluff past. As it is, possession will be the usual nine points, and slapping a herd through along Kingfisher will go a long way toward proving our point. It might even make them bow to the inevitable and leave us alone from now on."

"Now you're hopin' more than believin'," said Dusty Elliot, who'd been listening. "I think you're right about bringin' the cattle in, Dave. But as for that fact bluffin' Hendron and the Ballards into reformin' and bein' good dogs, uhn-uh! We're still goin' to have to do this the hard way."

"You," growled Kerchival, "are the damnedest pessimist. Anyway, Brace, you and Kirby could leave a couple of men apiece with us to help guard things, go make your gathers, and bring your cattle through. It will force the opposition's hand, one way or the other. What do you think?"

"We'll do it," declared Shotwell. "I'm of the mind right now to settle matters, once and for all, one way or another. I don't want to go through this same old argument every summer."

Kerchival turned to Joe Orchard and said softly: "For all we know, Joe, in that crowd that just rode away could be the man or men who killed Bill Yeager and Mel Rhodes."

"For all we know, mebbe." The deputy nodded. "But until we know, we'll keep on guessing. Here's something that may interest you, Dave. Lear Hendron has moved into the Starlight Hotel to live."

"Lear Hendron at the Starlight? How do you know, Joe? I mean, that she's moved there to live. Maybe she's just in town for a few days."

"All I know is what Hack Dinwiddie told me," said Joe. "He said she'd signed on for a room for a month in advance. And that she'd brought a fair amount of luggage. Hack figgers from the look in her eye an' the way she carried herself that she's split up with her father. Which is plumb understandable to me. She's a fine girl, Lear is . . . while that father of hers. . . ." Joe shook his head. "I've wondered more'n once how she'd stood for that cold-blooded, pompous, self-centered *hombre* all these years. And her brother Virg . . . he ain't much better than the old man when it comes to being an agreeable person to live around."

Kerchival built a cigarette. "If," he said thoughtfully, "Lear has really split up with her father, it could be because she has learned something that she just can't swallow . . . something that, if we knew it, could straighten out several things. I think I know Lear pretty well. She's not flighty, and it would take a pretty heavy jolt to cause her to leave her father. Sure would like to know what she knows."

"Why don't you try askin' her?" suggested Joe Orchard.

"Maybe I will," answered Kerchival.

CHAPTER THIRTEEN

The stars were so big and bright they seemed to be hanging almost at arm's length when Dave Kerchival and Joe Orchard rode into Warm Creek.

Brace Shotwell and Joe Kirby had left four of their men to bolster up Kerchival's little force and headed back to the plains with the rest. On leaving, Shotwell had said: "Look for us sometime between a week and ten days from now. You'll hear us coming with the cattle."

Joe Orchard turned his horse over to the care of Bus Spurgeon, but Dave Kerchival tied his at the rail in front of the Starlight Hotel. Abruptly he realized that this was the third horse in the past twenty-four hours he'd been on. The others he had ridden to a gaunt weariness. Now, also, weariness hit him like a club.

So much had happened in the space of these two dozen hours. Mel Rhodes had died under a killer's knife. He himself had rolled smoke against Shugrue, Abel Hendron's imported gunman. The Ballard headquarters had been pulled to pieces, and he had lost and regained possession of Lazy Y.

All these things had happened, but as yet Joe Orchard had no sure line at all on the killers of Bill Yeager and Mel Rhodes. And Bill Yeager's will was gone. Which left Dave Kerchival, hanging precariously onto a heritage that was his only if he could hold it. The fight was far from over—of that Kerchival was certain.

Kerchival stretched his big arms and shoulders, rubbed a

hand across his face, as though he would rub away the stiffness of fatigue that had settled there. He went into the Starlight where Hack Dinwiddie sat in the parlor with tipped-back chair and propped-up feet, browsing through a week-old copy of the Fort Devlin *Recorder.* Hack peered across the top of the paper.

"Don't tell me you let 'em bluff you out," growled Hack. "Heard you were having a mite of trouble out at Lazy Y. How about it?"

"They found the saddle a little too big and the horse too tall to ride this time," answered Kerchival dryly. "Hack, I'd like to talk to Lear Hendron."

"Sure." Hack nodded. "But mebbe she won't want to talk with you. Room Eighteen. She ain't left it since she arrived. Didn't even come down for supper."

Kerchival climbed the stairs, went along the hall, and knocked at the door of 18. He had to knock twice before an answer came, in a voice small and toneless.

"Yes? Who is it?"

"Dave Kerchival."

There was a stir of movement, the lock clicked, and the door opened. Lear Hendron was still in riding clothes. Her eyes were deep and dark, her face pale and set. The window shade was drawn and the lamp turned low. Kerchival knew a slight awkwardness when he spoke.

"Don't know whether I'm welcome or not, Lear, or if I can be of any help. But I wanted to make the offer, anyway."

She nodded and said: "Thank you. Please come in."

She indicated a chair and Kerchival sat there, twirling his hat in his hands. He leaned a little forward, watching her from beneath frowning, troubled brows. Lear sat on the edge of the bed, met his glance directly, and abruptly said: "I've left home, Dave. For good."

"Now," said Kerchival with some gentleness, "I don't like to

125

hear that and I hope you don't mean it, Lear. Home is always . . . home."

"For some perhaps," she said bitterly. "But not for me. You don't understand. Things had just become impossible."

She got to her feet with a sudden lithe twist of energy, and began pacing up and down the room. Words came from her almost fiercely.

"After . . . after my mother died, I never did know a real home. Oh, I tried to keep up a front, to make believe. But it was just a bluff, which I knew all the time and which suddenly I grew sick of. No, there wasn't any home. Just a place to live, that's all. Yet I might have stood for that if I could have done so while still keeping some small shred of my self-respect. But even that was denied me. It became hateful beyond endurance. . . ."

She broke off in her speaking but not her restless pacing. Kerchival laid his hat down, spun a cigarette into shape. He waited out the pause in silence. Presently her words came again.

"My father and brother . . . it's been like being in a house with strangers. Or with surly dogs, snapping at each other and at everything. Yet even that I might have been able to go on enduring, if it hadn't been for the wickedness that is there."

She paused beside the bed, sat down on it again. Dave Kerchival, watching her, wished she did not have that set, stunned look in her eyes. She rubbed a slim hand up the side of her face and across her dark curly head.

"You see, Dave," she said, with slow distinctness, "I'm convinced that my father knows all about the murder of Bill Yeager . . . and of Mel Rhodes. Oh, not that he fired the shot or used the knife . . . but he knows who did and expects to profit by it. And that makes him no better than . . . than the actual murderer. And, finally, there was this morning when he set that brute, Shugrue, on you. That was the final straw. I knew then that I couldn't stay another night in that house."

"That wasn't pretty," said Kerchival quietly. "I'm sorry you had to see it."

"I'm not," was her surprising answer. "I've been blind too long to too many things. If I'd had my eyes fully opened before, I'd have done long ago what I'm doing now . . . gone out on my own."

"What are your plans for the future, Lear?"

She shrugged. "They will come. I'm taking one step at a time. It's a new world I'm moving into. I must get used to it gradually."

A dozen useless comments cropped up in Kerchival's mind, but these were not the things he wanted to say at all. He wondered how much he dared ask this girl. . . . "You leave something half answered, Lear, that must be fully answered before you'll ever know an hour's mental peace again. There's got to be an answer to the deaths of Bill Yeager and Mel Rhodes. No matter who the final judgment rests on, we've got to have that answer. You say you're convinced your father knows who killed Bill Yeager and Mel Rhodes. What convinced you?"

She was still for a little time before answering. "It wasn't anything he said. More his manner, I guess. On hearing the news he was neither surprised nor sorry. It was as though he expected something of the sort and was satisfied when it happened." The hard, acid realism in Lear's tone and words jolted Kerchival. He found himself trying to find an excuse for Abel Hendron.

"We must remember that your father is a hard man to understand, Lear. So much of what he feels and thinks is never shown. He has a tighter rein on his emotions than most. Maybe we're misjudging him."

She lifted a hand and shook her dark head vehemently. "Please! That is the excuse I always made for him. I refuse to make it any longer. It . . . it was good of you to stop in, Dave."

Kerchival got up and moved to the door. "I don't know how or where this thing will end, Lear. But if there is anything at any time I can do for you, I want you to let me know."

She looked at him steadily. "You can do this for me. You can continue your fight, come what will, and no matter who you have to take arms against. For you are in the right. And I think it is going to be tremendously important to me to know that right can triumph. I'll . . . see you again?"

Kerchival nodded. "Yes, you'll see me again."

He closed the door softly and went down the hall, silently cursing Abel Hendron. The man deserved nothing now—nothing!

As Kerchival came off the bottom of the stairs and into the hotel parlor, he stopped short at sight of Hack Dinwiddie's barring Virg Hendron's way to the stairs and arguing with plenty of temper in his tone.

"Nothing doing, Virg," the hotelkeeper was saying. "You can't see her. When Lear took the room, she made me promise this . . . that I'd not let you or your father bother her. Maybe it was a fool's promise, but I made it and I'll keep it. Once and for all, you can't go up!"

Virg Hendron still bore signs of the whipping he had taken from Perk O'Dair, Kerchival noted. Virg's face was still puffed in places and dark-splotched with slowly fading bruises. Virg was furiously angry. "You can't stop me from seeing my own sister!" he stormed. "Get out of my way, Dinwiddie . . . before I. . . ."

"Before you what?" cut in Hack bluntly. "Virg, you should know better than to try and threaten anybody any more. The old Hendron fable is busted all to hell now. So right here and now I'm stopping you from bothering Lear. While it's her wish, that's the way it's going to be!"

Virg's fuming glance reached past Dinwiddie, settled on Kerchival. There was wildness in Virg's eyes, and uncertainty, and perhaps the awakening consciousness that life was not all an easy, secure groove for the spoiled, selfish son of a rich and powerful cattleman, that there were things he had taken for granted for so long that he had ceased to see them in their true importance and value until they were taken away from him.

"You!" he charged Kerchival thickly. "You've been up to see Lear. She would see you. And you're trying to tell me she won't see me . . . her brother? You're lying, Dinwiddie. You. . . ."

Kerchival moved right in on Virg, his face bleak, his eyes frosty. To Dinwiddie he said: "I'll take care of him, Hack." Then to Virg, as he dropped a hand on his shoulder: "You and me are taking a walk, my friend. I got things to say to you . . . plenty."

Virg tried to knock Kerchival's hand aside, but Kerchival's fingers dug in. He spun Virg around and drove him ahead out into the dark street. "If I thought it was worth the effort," said Kerchival harshly, "I'd take on where Perk O'Dair left off, Virg. I'd whip hell out of you. But no matter how much you beat jelly, you can't make iron out of it, so we'll forego that pleasure. But now I'm going to tell you a few things, and you damned well better listen."

Kerchival marched Virg clear down to Bus Spurgeon's livery corrals before he got his temper under sufficient control to talk with reasonable evenness.

"You don't deserve a thing, Virg. You'd better start understanding that, once and for all. Any kind of a break that you get from here on out you want to be damned thankful for, because you sure don't rate any. You've given your sister a rotten deal. You've been so cussed selfish and spoiled you never bothered to think of anybody but yourself. When, I wonder, did you ever think of her, consider her life and happiness? Never, I guess . . . until maybe now, just a little. I saw it in your eyes, back there at the hotel. You've lost something, haven't you, Virg? Something

129

that has walked right out of your life. Your sister, who, up until now, you just took for granted. Virg . . . you've been a poor, miserable fool."

Virg wasn't protesting Kerchival's grip on his shoulder now. He wasn't protesting anything, or saying anything, either; his angry muttering had quieted.

Kerchival went on remorselessly: "Lear put something into War Hatchet that kept it a faint semblance of a home, didn't she, Virg? She gave so much for you and your father, and stood for so much. Until finally she just couldn't give any more or stand any more. While you took and took and took and gave nothing in return. So now she's gone. And you're scared, Virg. Lear represented something to cling to, didn't she? Something fine and good and true. But now she's not there any more and there's a hell of a frightening gap in your life. Well, Virg, you're going to go home and leave Lear alone. Right now she's got things to think out and she wants to arrive at the answers in her own way. I don't know if she'll ever want to see you again. If she ever does, she'll send for you. And when and if she ever does, then you better come to her on your hands and knees. For she is that far above you."

Kerchival took his hand off Virg's arm. Virg never said a word. He headed upstreet to his horse, swung into the saddle, and rode out of town.

There was a light in Joe Orchard's office. Kerchival went over there. The deputy was alone at his desk, slouched deeply in his chair, his weary eyes half-lidded and brooding. He jerked his head toward a chair, brought a bottle and glasses from a desk drawer.

"If it'd do any good," he growled, "I'd get drunk. As it is, have a short one with me, Dave. Never felt so useless in my life. Good men die, the tough way, and I can't find a single answer."

"This afternoon I saw a strange thing," said Kerchival slowly.

"I've done a lot of thinking about it since and it doesn't add up. See what you can do with it, Joe."

He went on to tell of seeing Abel Hendron and Jack Tully out in the little meadow beyond Kingfisher Creek. "I was surprised to see Jack Tully out and riding and surprised to see him talking with Hendron. And then to see Hendron go for his gun and see Tully beat him to it and hold the drop . . . I thought sure Tully was going to shoot, but he didn't. So there's something else for you to browse on, Joe."

"You damned sure you saw all that?" demanded Orchard.

Kerchival grinned with crooked mirthlessness. "I guess I did, Joe. It came to me at the time that I must be seeing things. But I blinked my eyes a couple of times and took another look. And it was all real enough."

Joe Orchard poured a quarter of an inch of whiskey into his glass, swilled it around and around while staring at it. "From what I've seen of Jack Tully, he ain't one to ride much. Mostly he seems to like the idea of sitting on the bench by Sam Lieder-man's store door and watchin' the world go by. Still and all, there's no law against his forking a saddle if the idea hit him. He could have bumped into Hendron by accident. But why would Hendron try and throw a gun on him?"

"That," said Kerchival dryly, "is one question I couldn't find the answer to. So I'm asking you."

Orchard grunted. "He was on War Hatchet range. Maybe Hendron was just ordering him off. With things going the way they are, mebbe Hendron figured he was spyin', or something. Oh, hell! Seems like all I can do is figure mebbe this . . . mebbe that."

"I was going to suggest that we look up Jack Tully and ask him why," drawled Kerchival.

Joe Orchard drained his glass and got to his feet. "Come on!"

Jack Tully lived in a little cabin at the outskirts of town. It was dark when Dave Kerchival and Joe Orchard came up to it. Joe knocked solidly on the door several times without getting an answer. He tried the latch and the door opened easily. Joe called once—"Hey, Tully!"—but got no answer to that, either. Joe scratched a match, nursed it to its widest flare, then crossed to a table and lit the small lamp standing there. By the light of this they looked around. The cabin showed indubitable signs of recent usage, but at the same time now gave off another impression, the feeling of a cage from which a bird had flown. There were no blankets on the bunk, and what had been a grub shelf above the stove was bare, except for a few odds and ends that didn't amount to much. A dishpan and an old galvanized boiler hung on nails driven into the wall, but all cooking utensils were gone.

"This," said Joe Orchard, "is queer . . . damned queer. By the signs, Jack Tully has up and left town."

"If he has," said Kerchival, "he didn't walk. Let's go see Bus Spurgeon."

The livery owner was propped up on a bunk in his harness room, a lamp at his elbow, reading a dog-eared veterinary manual. To Kerchival's question, he nodded and laid aside his book. "Sure, Dave. Jack Tully's owned a bronco for some time now. Bought it from me two or three months ago. Kept it here, along with his ridin' gear. Said he was gettin' tired of sittin' around all the time and yearned to feel a bronco under him again. Jack's an old cavalry trooper, you know. Every now and then he'd go out for a ride, generally in the early mornin' or late evenin'. Thought you knew that."

"No, I didn't know it . . . until today," Kerchival said. "About him taking to riding, I mean. Fact is, I never did give much thought to Tully, one way or the other . . . always figured him sort of a town loafer and let it go at that. Though I did wonder a couple of times where he got enough money to live on."

"Reckon he draws some sort of pension or retirement pay," put in Joe Orchard. "Being an old soldier, he would."

Bus Spurgeon looked at them keenly. "Why you two interested?"

"Just wondering," murmured Kerchival. "His horse and riding gear here now?"

Bus shook his head. "He rode out pretty early this afternoon. Ain't come back yet." The stable owner's eyes pinched down suddenly. "Don't tell me you think somethin's happened to Jack?"

"What could happen to him?" grunted Joe Orchard.

"Shucks, I dunno. But after Bill Yeager and Mel Rhodes, how's a man goin' to figger anything?"

"That's right . . . how is he?" said Kerchival, moving to the door. "Obliged, Bus."

Out in the dark of the street Kerchival built a smoke and frowned wearily at the stars. "I'm going home and get some sleep, Joe. If I try and think any more now, I'll bust a cinch."

"Before you leave, answer me one question," growled the deputy. "Abel Hendron and Jack Tully are both ex-cavalrymen. Did they know each other before they came into this country?"

Kerchival inhaled deeply, blew invisible smoke through pursed lips. "That I wouldn't know. But I'm wondering, just like you."

CHAPTER FOURTEEN

At War Hatchet headquarters weary saddle mounts lined the corral fence. In the ranch house, under lamps that seemed to throw out a sullen glow, Abel Hendron faced the Ballards and three outside riders. Gard Ballard was pacing the floor, raging.

"What did we find when we got home? A mess. Everything pulled to pieces. Lefty, the cook, gone. No answer to anything. If I'd known they'd done that to us, I'd never have walked out of Lazy Y headquarters peaceable. I'd have shot it out with Kerchival and his crowd to the last damned cartridge."

"And ended up as dead as Al Shugrue and Ben Factor," said one of the outside riders harshly. "Me, I haven't been in these parts long, but I can see one thing plain! You've been too damn' sure of yourselves. You've underestimated somebody, this fellow Kerchival in particular. He's been thinkin' out ahead of you at every jump."

Gard Ballard beat a clenched fist at empty air. "He ain't so smart, Shacks. He's just been lucky, so far."

"Lucky, nothin'," retorted Shacks. "Smart, I tell you. Right now he's got Lazy Y again. What you got? Not even a headquarters. One thing you better realize right now, Ballard. There's got to be better headwork runnin' this deal if I'm to stay in it."

Spence Ballard turned on the speaker. "What's the matter, Shacks, lost your guts? Aimin' to coyote on us, maybe?"

Shacks looked Spence up and down. "You got my permission to test my nerve any time you've a mind to, friend . . . right

134

now, if you feel that way. What I been talkin' about ain't a question of nerve or no nerve, but a question of plain damn' common sense. To lick a man, you got to outthink him, first. I'll ride a tough trail to a finish any time and anywhere, providin' my side is showin' as much brainwork as the other. But I don't ride blind in damn' foolishness. Now you know."

Gard Ballard would have had more to say, but Abel Hendron headed him off.

"Shacks is right," said Hendron, coldly precise. "We have made the major mistake of underestimating the opposition. I am as guilty there as anyone else, perhaps more so. My mistake was in seeing Dave Kerchival as merely a cowhand who used to work for me. I saw him as one who for five years took my orders and obeyed them. For that reason I did not see the man in his true stature. He is no fool and he can be ruthless and deadly. I saw him kill Al Shugrue, after Shugrue had all the edge. It wasn't luck. We must revise our thinking and our plan of battle."

"Now," said Shacks, "we're gettin' somewhere."

Gard Ballard squared around to face Hendron. "You got this . . . plan of battle?"

"Yes. It will be this way."

For fifteen minutes Abel Hendron spoke without interruption. When he had finished, Shacks said: "That makes sense. You don't win a tough hand by bettin' peanuts."

"Joe Orchard," growled Gard Ballard, "will favor Kerchival, same as he has from the first."

"Joe Orchard doesn't count," said Hendron coldly. "He'll be treated like anyone else who gets in our way. You'll all headquarter here, of course."

They trooped out, put up their horses, and found sleeping quarters for themselves. Left alone, Abel Hendron lighted a long black cheroot and prowled the room restlessly. The lamplight cut his face into hard angles and flat shadows, and a strange heat beat in his unrelenting eyes.

This man could not stand to be thwarted in anything, could not bear to have his domination questioned. All his life the privilege of absolute authority had been his fetish, the vital prop to his entire existence. It had been his greatest strength. It was something he needed to hold him together. It was the mainstay of his blind, unreasoning pride. It made him big in his own eyes, fed his ego.

For years that authority had never been questioned. As a cavalry officer he had been a ruthless martinet, and men under him could not answer back or question him then. As a civilian cattleman he had made that same authority stick for many years. Some men had been cowed by it, but now that domination was beginning to break up.

Dave Kerchival had looked at him, laughed at him, thrown his authority back in his face. The rest of his crew had, in effect, done the same, and followed Kerchival away. And, finally, rebellion had arisen in the last place he'd ever expected it: from his own children. From Lear, his daughter, who had left the onerous shelter of his roof. And from Virg, his son, who, though still staying on at the ranch, was getting out from under his hand. And for these latter things, Abel Hendron knew no answer.

Dave Kerchival and other men he could fight in his own way. But what could he do about Lear—about Virg? Virg he might still handle. But Lear?

Men would hear about Lear. That kind of news would spread quickly. And when next Abel Hendron rode into Warm Creek, men would look at him with sardonic eyes, would laugh openly. They would scorn the authority he had worked to spread across all of the Mount Cherokee plateau range, because they would see that such authority no longer existed even in his own home. Men would ridicule him, and no authority could stand against ridicule. Such things had brought about the downfall of empires.

These thoughts and realizations were gall and wormwood to Abel Hendron. They burned in him like acid and cut bitter, savage lines into the hard mask of his face. He was still pacing the room when Virg came home.

Virg closed the door behind him, put his shoulders against the wall, and stared at his father with hostile eyes. Hendron came around on him harshly.

"Well . . . did you see her?"

"No," answered Virg tonelessly. "No, I didn't."

"Why not? That's what you rode to town for, wasn't it?"

Virg drew a deep breath. "She didn't want to see me. And she doesn't want to see you, either. She asked Hack Dinwiddie to see that neither of us bothered her."

Abel Hendron ground his teeth. "That don't make sense. She can't deny. . . ."

"She doesn't want to see us," cut in Virg. "Whether it does or doesn't make sense to you, that's the way it is. She won't see us. But she did see and talk with Dave Kerchival. Figure that one out."

Something came into Abel Hendron's expression that Virg had never seen before, something that shocked Virg and made him grow white about the lips. It was as though his father had become a complete stranger to him, and a wicked one.

"The little fool!" cried Abel Hendron harshly. "She would do that to me . . . her father? For that I'll. . . ."

"No, you won't." Virg pushed away from the wall, moved up to a short stride's distance. He was taller than his father and now seemed somehow to loom over him. There was haggardness in Virg, but also now a sudden and new-found strength about his mouth and chin. He spoke bluntly. "No matter what Lear decides to do, you'll leave her alone. You won't threaten anything and you'll keep your tongue off her. Kerchival's right. Lear is so far above you or me we can't even stand in her shadow. We've both lost the only thing in our lives that was worth a damn. And the fault is ours, not Lear's. Keep your tongue off her!"

Father and son stood, glances locked. And each was seeing the other in a hard new light. If the ravening hunger for personal domination had not been so consuming a thing in Abel Hendron, he might have known a deep pride in Virg at that moment. For the sulky, sullen wastrel son was suddenly a man, cold-eyed, unafraid, and master of the situation. Hard and racking reality had burned the soft dross out of Virg. He had come up out of somewhere to stand on the level, his own man. But what he saw in his father left him empty and old inside.

Once more he said: "You'll keep your tongue off her." Then he turned and walked steadily out of the room.

Virg was up early the next morning. He hadn't slept too well. In fact, he hadn't slept at all until after midnight. For a long time the trail of life had been easy. Then it had grown rough and rugged. And abruptly Virg found himself at a fork in that trail of which he somehow knew the correct evaluation meant everything for all his future years. He had to take the right fork, for there could be no turning back if he took the wrong one.

It was a case of casting up all accounts, of facing every truth, no matter how bleak and bitter it might be. These things he must do. And in the still darkness of his room he did these things and came to his decision and finally knew some peace of mind and then sleep because of it.

In the gray, moist dawn he crossed to the cook shack, washed up, and then stood backed up to a corner of the stove and watched silently as Deaf Blair got breakfast together. Virg was eating when the Ballards and the three outside riders came in.

These men, in particular the Ballards, were part and parcel of a scheme of things that Virg had suddenly come to hate.

Cousins of his they might be, and companions of many of his past years. But just as he was seeing many other things now in a brand-new light, so he saw the Ballards at this moment.

Gard, rough and domineering, crudely intolerant. Spence, coldly sneering, wicked of eye. And Turk, nearer his own age than either of the others, aping the worst of both his brothers and adding to it a streak of the blustering bully. Yes, at this moment Virg Hendron saw the Ballards very clearly for exactly what they were, and understood fully his sister's antipathy toward them.

Gard and Spence paid him small attention, a contemptuous indifference that set little fires burning in Virg. But Turk wasn't satisfied with this—the bully's roughness had to assert itself. He straddled the bench beside Virg, put both hands on Virg's shoulder, and gave him a sudden, heavy push.

"Get over, dear cousin. You take up too much room!"

Virg had been sitting at the end of the bench. Expecting nothing of this sort, he had no chance to brace himself. He went off the bench and piled up on the floor. Turk doubled over, howling with laughter.

Virg came up fast, blind with fury. He set himself and swung, putting his fist solidly home to the side of Turk's face, knocking him half across the table, where he stayed for a moment, half dazed. Then, cursing instead of laughing, Turk hauled away from the table, forgot he was astride the bench, tripped over it, and went down on his hands and knees. But he came up with a rush and dived at Virg, who went in to meet him, both fists swinging.

They met chest to chest and wasted a lot of wild but muffled punches. Then Turk got an arm around Virg's neck, tried to get a hip under him and wrestle him down. They reeled and staggered back and forth without any advantage either way. They banged into the wall, bounced off it, broke apart.

Turk brought in an overhand swing that caught Virg high on the forehead, knocking him back, shaken and hurt. Quick to follow his advantage, Turk landed another under the eye, and Virg went down. Turk charged in, ready to use his boots, and Deaf Blair, watching this thing, reached for an iron skillet. But Turk got no chance to use his boots. Some instinct told Virg what to do. He rolled over and threw himself toward Turk's churning feet, muffled the half-started kick, and brought Turk down with a crash. Then Virg was back on his feet as quickly as Turk had managed it.

Virg was amazed at how good he felt. Those punches had knocked him down, sent crazy lights exploding before his eyes. But now, amazingly enough, that effect was entirely gone and his head was clear. He wasn't afraid of anything, and the juices of a boundless, clamoring strength flowed all through him. He couldn't wait to get on with this thing.

He saw Turk start another of those clubbing, overhand swings, went in under it, and drove his fist to Turk's mouth with the full roll of his shoulder and the drive of his body behind it. The punch stopped Turk's steady, aimless cursing as abruptly as a cork slapped into a bottle.

It was the hardest punch Virg Hendron had ever thrown in his life and it hurt Turk Ballard badly. It made a pouting, bloody mess of his lips and drove him back two full strides where, for a moment, he rocked and reeled, his legs going rubbery.

Realization of what he had done and what he could do was a galvanizing current in Virg. He laughed without knowing he did so, a low, cold sound, supremely confident, and moved in on Turk with a slithering, prowling stride. He feinted a left at Turk's beaten mouth and, when Turk's hands went up to ward off the blow, pivoted low and dug his right fist deep into Turk's body. He felt Turk's belly muscles quiver and sag, heard Turk's grunting gasp of agony. And as Turk started to double over, Virg straightened and clubbed him twice on the jaw. Turk went down. Deaf Blair, a silent man little given to words, cackled shrilly: "Boot him, boy . . . boot him! He'd 'a' done it to you. Boot him!"

Nobody paid any attention to Deaf except Spence Ballard, who jerked around, a hard snarl on his lips, which bothered old Deaf not a bit. Deaf waved his skillet recklessly and yelled again: "Boot him, boy!"

Instead, Virg waited for Turk to get up, leaning a little forward, knees slightly bent, fists clenched and ready-swinging. Turk was in no rush to get back to his feet. He half lay, half sat on the floor, chin sagging loosely while he gulped and blubbered for air. His eyes rolled up at Virg, black with hate. He lurched to one knee and went for his gun.

Virg pounced, caught Turk's wrist, swung his arm over and back with a savage jerk. Turk yelled crazily and dropped his gun. Virg hauled him to his feet, threw him against the wall, and spoke for the first time.

"You damned, blustering yellow whelp!"

Then his fists started swinging again. Twice Turk tried to lunge away from the wall and twice Virg knocked him back with winging punches. Turk's head began to roll, and a sagging looseness made him soft all over. Virg finished it with another crushing smash to the mouth. Turk piled up on the floor against the wall, moaning and helpless.

Virg turned and faced the room. A trickle of crimson seeped from one nostril. One eye was swelling and there was a savage redness on his forehead where Turk's best punch had landed. Gard Ballard was staring at him with the expression of one who had just seen something that wasn't possible. Spence was glaring, hating him. Deaf Blair was grinning from ear to ear.

To Gard Ballard, Virg said: "Tell him that from now on when he meets me he's to tip his hat."

With that Virg stepped past Turk and went out.

Dawn's grayness was turning to old rose and ashes of pearl along the eastern sky. Abel Hendron, with his stiff, precise stride, was coming across from the ranch house.

"What's going on out here?" he rapped. "Did I hear somebody yell?"

"Yeah," answered Virg, equally curt, "you did. I just whipped hell out of Turk Ballard."

Virg moved past his father and on to the corrals. He shook out a rope and caught up a bronco. He saddled and swung astride. The cold morning air felt good as it stung his bruised face. He headed for town.

CHAPTER FIFTEEN

At Lazy Y headquarters affairs fell into a fairly contented pattern, leavened with an air of watchful waiting. With everybody pitching in, including the men Brace Shotwell had left, work on the new bunkhouse went ahead fast. Logs were felled and peeled, snaked to location, notched, and skidded into place. The walls rose, rafters were cut and fitted, and split shakes nailed into place.

From time to time Dave Kerchival and Dusty Elliot would saddle up and ride a careful patrol, reading all trails for signs. At night, guard shifts watched the dark hours through. Kerchival was taking no chances on being surprised or caught off guard.

As the days drifted by without untoward incident, Perk O'Dair expressed the opinion that Abel Hendron and the Ballards had decided to let well enough alone. But Dusty Elliot knocked this juvenile hope on the head brusquely.

"We go playin' with that idea and we'll lose our shirts," declared Dusty. "Abel Hendron won't ever quit tryin' to boss the universe until he's dead or busted up so bad he ain't got a leg to stand on. So far, he ain't either. And if you think the Ballards have turned to sweetness and light, you're crazy, boy. They're cookin' up somethin', and one of these days you'll know what it's all about. In the meantime it'll pay us to keep lookin' an' listenin'."

Joe Orchard dropped by a couple of times and reported to

Kerchival that so far he hadn't picked up a trace of Jack Tully.

"Just like he'd vanished into thin air," grumbled the deputy. "And it doesn't add up. Men like Tully don't just up and fly the coop without a damn' good reason. Only way I can figger it is that after his little ruckus with Abel Hendron, Tully lost his nerve and decided to leave the country. But somehow that doesn't reason out right, either. Jack Tully was the sort that stayed pretty much to himself with nobody getting to know him very well. But from what I saw of him, I'd have read Tully as a man who didn't scare easy."

"My judgment of him," agreed Kerchival. "There's an angle there, Joe, that could be plenty important, if we could just put a finger on it. We'll just have to wait it out. Something may break."

"Here's something to interest you," said Joe. "I dropped in at War Hatchet the other day. Not a soul around but the cook, Deaf Blair. Me an' Deaf had a cup of coffee together and Deaf told me a few things. The Ballards and those three outside riders are headquartering at War Hatchet now. Deaf said everybody seemed to be waiting for something, but he didn't know what. Told me something else, too. The other morning Turk Ballard got fresh with Virg Hendron and Virg licked the whey outta him. Deaf said he couldn't hardly believe his eyes the way Virg tore into Turk. And Deaf says that Virg doesn't take a thing from the old man. If Virg ain't all of a sudden growed into a pretty good man, he's showing all the signs, so Deaf claims."

"Why not?" Kerchival nodded. "Virg is Lear Hendron's brother. If he grows to be even half as good a man as she is a woman, he'll stack up aces high. Life's caught up with Virg. When that happens to a fellow like Virg, it either makes or breaks him. For Lear's sake I hope it's the first."

Came a day when a long, low banner of tawny dust built up on the plains and moved steadily up toward the hill country. Under that dust banner plodded hundreds of white-faced cattle.

Riders rode at point, at flank, and at drag. The herd passed the town of Warm Creek a full mile to the east, its voiced complaint a dull rumble that carried steadily across the interval. It met the first upsweep and flowed up it, a living river of shifting color.

A rider spurred well out ahead of it and came racking in to Lazy Y headquarters. To Kerchival he said: "Shotwell and Kirby got a thousand head coming in on the Kingfisher trail. The trail still open?"

"Still open and we'll keep it so," Kerchival told him. "We'll be on hand."

The rider spurred back the way he had come. Kerchival and Dusty Elliot and the four plainsmen who had been staying at Lazy Y caught and saddled. Perk O'Dair and Chick Roland were to stay at headquarters and keep an eye on things. Kerchival grinned at them.

"Don't let the same fire burn you in the same place again," he cautioned.

The two young riders squirmed. "Anybody comes snoopin' they'll run into somethin'," vowed Perk.

Kerchival and the others rode down to meet the herd. Brace Shotwell had just moved up from the drag, his weather-beaten face grim under a coating of dust.

"So far so good," he said. "But what's ahead? Got a feeling about this drive. We put it through, it should prove something to Abel Hendron and the Ballards. Which is that we don't intend to be stopped . . . not ever."

"Haven't heard a squeak out of them since we run 'em off Lazy Y, Brace," said Kerchival. "Either they've decided the game ain't worth the candle or they're storing up something. We'll see."

At War Hatchet headquarters things were on the move, men catching and saddling. Spence Ballard was switching his saddle from a horse, sweating and blown from hard running, to a fresh mount. While he worked at it, he reported over his shoulder to Abel Hendron in his curt, thin-lipped way.

"You had it figgered right. The plains crowd are bringing in a herd. Right on a thousand head is my guess. And moving up Kingfisher, of course."

A boiling shine reflected from Hendron's hard brown eyes. "This is something we should have done long ago. Our mistake has been talking instead of acting. We'll correct that mistake today. I'm glad it's a big herd."

"Herd that size is hard to stop," growled a rider. "Hard to turn, hard to handle, once it starts running wild."

"Anything runs downhill better than up," said Hendron. "If you had your choice, where would you rather be, above or below when a thousand cattle begin to run?"

"Above, of course."

"Exactly. That's where we'll be. The other side will be below."

The pace of the herd slowed, for here nearly every step of the way was up. To some extent the solid mass of the herd broke up, shortening and widening. For here there was timber to thread through and there was the run of the creek waters, splashing and cool, to lure thirsty stragglers from the red-and-white ranks. And there were always others that fought the labor of the climb and tried to swing away at easier traveled angles that would take them around the swing of the slope instead of up it. So the work of men and horses increased steadily.

Only two riders were left at point; all the rest were working the flanks and the drag. The complaint of the herd deepened, a steady rumble along the ridges and under the timber. Masses of cattle broke and spread and moved in scattered lines through the timber, to meet and mass again on some bench or small clearing and then break up once more into plodding files that wound and twisted and moved ever on and higher.

Cutting sharp and shrill above the herd's complaint was the *hi-yiing* and *yipping* of the riders. Sweating ponies nudged laggards and reata ends thumped stubborn bovine ribs. Men and horses raced into sudden movement to head off stragglers and stretches of the creek waters boiled under the lunge and lash of hoofs.

Much of the underfoot was forest mold, deep and thick and muffling, but on the steeper ridge sides was hard earth that, chopped and beaten by hundreds of hoofs, sent up a dust that swirled in amber sluggishness through the sun-drenched timber and across the glades.

Dave Kerchival, working the flanks and the drag, wherever his cowhand's instinct and knowledge told him special effort was needed, saw Lazy Y cattle begin to mingle with Brace Shotwell's Flat S and Joe Kirby's K in a Box brands. It was always thus, he knew, when a big herd moved through other cattle country. A big herd seemed to carry a sort of suction with it, pulling in strays and smaller bands.

In this case it did not matter. Lazy Y stuff always moved up to the loftier summer range as the season advanced. And in the fall, when the big gather was made, the brands would be sorted out and drifted back to their proper range.

The main chore was to get this herd beyond the rim and onto the plateau's lush vastness, and now a nagging sense of urgency began to work on Dave Kerchival, pulling at his nerve ends and sharpening the lines of his face.

For Abel Hendron was bound to know about this herd and its destination. It was the thing that Hendron had, for the past several years, worked to prevent—the movement of the plains herds to and from the high summer range. As long as it went on, there could be no permanent joining up of War Hatchet and Ballard range, and without that permanent joining Hendron's fanatic dream of complete control of the Mount Cherokee plateau would remain an empty one.

The death of Bill Yeager was definitely tied in somewhere to that dream of empire, as was that of Mel Rhodes. And unless Hendron and his renegade nephews had decided to give up their hope of control, then they would have to do something about this herd. And Kerchival could not bring himself to believe that Hendron had decided to call it quits—the man simply wasn't made that way. The Ballards might falter and weaken, but Hendron never would. He was a man driven.

Kerchival sought out Brace Shotwell and told him of his unease. "Maybe I read more into Abel Hendron than is there, Brace . . . maybe all the things that have happened have got me shying at shadows . . . but I can't believe that Hendron has folded. Maybe he has. Maybe the fact that Lear has left War Hatchet and that Virg is showing signs of bucking over the traces has finally brought him to his senses. Maybe he's at last come to realize that he's losing far more than he could ever gain. But somehow I don't believe he's seen the light. The man is too damned self-centered, too selfish, too completely given to the idea of rule or ruin. And with that being so, he can't afford to let us put this herd through without a fight. If he does, he admits he's licked, and once he admits that, he'll have little luck getting enough support to carry on the fight. Even the Ballards will quit following him. A man like Hendron can't afford to lose, ever."

Shotwell, rubbing sweat and dust from his face, stared up toward the crest.

"We're better than halfway there. Give us another couple of hours and there won't be anything Hendron can do. I'm wondering how much of Hendron's past toughness has been bluff and how much backbone. I've seen more than one strutter come apart at the hinges when his bluff is really called . . .

called cold. Yet we'd be fools not to take some precaution, Dave. A little scout up ahead wouldn't hurt."

"My thought." Kerchival nodded. "I'll do it."

He swung wide, getting beyond the last fringe of the herd before setting his horse to a lunging climb. He worked up the nose of a ridge and threaded the thinning timber along the backbone of it. From here, through breaks in the timber, he could catch a clear view of the rim and the funneled pass that broke through it and led to the plateau's wide crest.

Up there the solid mass of the timber ran out into ragged patches and tongues licking into shale and slide-rock country, with aspens and chokecherry and scrub mahogany taking over in mottled belts below the rim. Lofty and austere and lonely ran the rim, its crest bright-etched against the sunlit sky, but with blue-black shadows blocked in below the overhangs. A buzzard drifted on motionless wings, skimming the crest, following its every jut and curve as though drawn by some invisible force.

Kerchival pushed on up until he'd reached the last edge of timber and saw nothing or heard nothing above. From below lifted the voice of the herd and the far-off shrill crying of the men who drove it. Faint as distant smoke, thin dust haze sifted above the timber.

Dave Kerchival built a cigarette, deciding there had been nothing to his fears. And knew better the next second. Something struck home with a wicked thock, and his horse staggered and shook all over. From the center of the sweaty shoulder just ahead of his right knee, Kerchival saw bright crimson begin to pour.

And then the horse was going down, crumpling, something breaking to pieces, all at once.

CHAPTER SIXTEEN

In the gray, chill early morning gloom under the Mount Cherokee rim, Jack Tully stirred in his blankets, found no further comfort in them, so rolled out and pulled on his boots, cursing the air's stark bite. In the banked ashes of last night's fire he found a few live coals that he tucked together before stacking dry aspen twigs on them. On hands and knees Tully bent and blew on the coals, and they brightened and set the twigs to smoking. Presently a thread of flame licked up, and Tully added larger wood.

For a time he hunkered there, shoulders hunched, drawing in the welcome heat of the flames. His face was frowsy with unshaven whiskers, a graying stubble that made it look as though his jaw were dusted with fire ashes. Under that stubble the pudginess of his features had fallen into slack lines that put wattles under his chin and loose folds across his cheeks and left his nose jutting in a strangely beaked effect. But his eyes burned coldly and, even here in this spot of solitary isolation, held their own dark secretiveness.

Presently he straightened, carried a smoke-blackened coffee pot over to a water seep, brought it back dripping, and pushed it into the edge of the flames. From a well-filled gunny sack he dug out a side of bacon, cut several slices from it, and spread them in a frying pan. At the edge of the aspen thicket that walled off this camp on the lower side, his horse greeted him with a soft whicker.

Jack Tully had selected this camp with care. Here he was hidden from any view except from the rest of the rim, directly above, and discovery from there at this particular time and season was highly unlikely. Nothing but the driest of dead aspen wood went on his fire, which gave off little smoke, and this, by the time it had slithered and winnowed its way to the crest of the rim, had dissolved into nothingness.

Tully ate his breakfast, drank his coffee. Then he rolled and smoked two cigarettes while the fire died and fell to ashes. After which he prowled off to the side some fifty yards where a narrow chimney ran part way up the rim's flank, climbed this as high as he could go, and from here watched day take over all the vast sweep of country below. He saw the sun's first blaze sweep in from the east, gilding the timber tops away down there, saw night's haze and cold shadows shrink and vanish.

There was a certain Indian-like patience and stoicism in Jack Tully. He was a man who could stay still and watchful for hours at a time and he stayed that way now, turning over in his mind the problems that drove and maneuvered men down in that country below him, and something sardonic pinched his eye corners and his lips curled.

Abel Hendron, with his false front of stiff-necked pride and arrogance and his overweening lust for range and power. Dave Kerchival, throwing a challenge squarely in the path of that drive for domination. The Ballards, roistering, stupid pawns in Abel Hendron's game. Men of the plains, like Brace Shotwell and Joe Kirby, whipping themselves to earn a tough living out of a tough world.

All such as these sitting in on a no-limit game and so busy hating and distrusting each other they were missing the easier way of skimming the cream from the milk pot. Jack Tully would take care of that. He was picking the top cards from the deck, the cards men would pay big money for. Right now there was some discomfort, but this would pass. In the end he would collect, for he was smart enough to move into a spot where he could play one against the other.

So mused Jack Tully as he crouched with the solid bulk of the Mount Cherokee rim at his back and watched the world below.

As the sun climbed ever higher and the stride of day lengthened, Tully began to see things. First, away, away down there where the dark belt of timber ended at the edge of the plains, there was dust, a solid banner of it, and Tully was wise enough to know what that dust meant. Cattle on the move, a lot of them. And for this, only one answer. Plains cattle, moving in on the drive for summer range. Tully stirred slightly. This could mean action. Tully's eyes sharpened with interest.

Later, Tully saw something else that pulled him around and set him up, taut and alert. Off to the east and high up, where the timber ran out into the shale country and the brush belt below the rim, the sun had struck up several bright flashes, glinting on metal. Riders out there, a good dozen of them. Tully saw them top a ridge, then drop from sight into an aspen-choked gulch. They did not reappear.

Tully left his point of vantage, returned to his camp, brought up his horse, and saddled it. Then, moving on foot and leading the animal, he worked a cautious way to the west, hugging the base of the rim, using the brush that bulked against it for cover. He kept to this way for a full mile before finding what he wanted, a gulch that funneled down from the rim base to the first reaches of timber below. He kept to the bottom of the gulch, still afoot, until the cover of the timber closed about him. Then he mounted and headed east again, riding with great care and caution.

In time he picked up the first faint echoes of activity ahead and below him—the rumbling complaint of driven cattle, the thin, high cutting yelps of riders. Now he dismounted, left his horse in a thick patch of jack pines, drew his rifle from its saddle boot, and prowled off afoot, a pudgy shapeless man, frowsy under the sagging brim of his down-pulled hat, and with sweat starting easily to lay a dark stain through his faded shirt across the mull of his shoulders.

If he had figured this thing right, and Tully was sure that he had, battle lay ahead. Plains cattle coming up the trail and Hendron's crowd climbing high to get above the herd and block it off from Mount Cherokee. Yeah, battle between the fools, and, if a smart man hung around the edges of a thing of this sort and used his head, there was no telling what kind of valuable cards he might draw.

In time he found a place that suited him, where he was securely hidden and from which he could watch. It was from the edge of a timber patch, and here he hunkered down, rubbing the sweat from his face with a grimy shirt sleeve, then building and nursing a cigarette.

The tumult from below grew steadily louder as the herd climbed ever higher. And presently there was a single rider, drifting through scattered timber along a ridge top, finally to break into the clear at the edge of the brush area. A good four hundred yards distant, that rider was, but Tully recognized him. Dave Kerchival.

He saw Kerchival rein up, stand tall in his stirrups as he looked over the country above. He saw Kerchival settle back in his saddle. Then he saw Kerchival's horse lurch and stagger and go down. While, from the slope above, thin and hard and venomous, echoed the ringing voice of a rifle. . . .

With his mount falling away beneath him, Dave Kerchival started to shuck himself from the saddle, instinctively going out the near side. Which was a mistake, for, as his horse had been standing, that was the downhill side. And though Kerchival landed clear on this first jump, the stricken horse rolled with the slope and its limp bulk struck Kerchival and knocked him spinning. He crashed headlong into the timber fringe, the side of his head slamming into a tree. He crumpled down there, half stunned. At the far edge of his wavering consciousness he caught the dimming echoes of a rifle shot.

It seemed to Kerchival that some tremendous interval of time must have passed while he lay there helpless. Yet all the time clamoring instincts were telling him he had to be up and doing something about this. He rolled over on his face, dug in his toes, and lurched to his knees. The world was still spinning crazily and he fell flat again. But there was a deep toughness in him that got him up to his knees again and then to his feet, a hand against the tree holding him up and steadying him.

There, only a couple of yards above him, lay his horse, still twitching. Jutting from under it was the stock of his rifle. He lurched forward, caught at the weapon, and pulled. It gave so easily that he went off balance again and dropped to one knee. But all he held in his hand was the rifle stock. The weight of the horse, in falling and rolling, had broken the stock clean across at the grip. Except for his belt gun he had no weapon.

He dropped the broken rifle stock, began to dodge back along the timbered ridge top, then dived for the shelter of a small thicket. For coming down from the slope above was the slash and pound of racing riders and a hard voice yelling: "Get into it! Get into it!"

They went by him within twenty yards and he wondered how they missed seeing him. The Ballards—Gard and Spence and Turk. Abel Hendron, and several strange riders. A small avalanche of men and riders, weaving and dodging and slamming on through the timber. Then they were gone, leaving behind the piney breath of churned-up forest mold and the hot odors of laboring horseflesh.

Down where the point of the herd was, Kerchival heard a

single high yell of alarm and warning, a yell that cut off abruptly in a quick spattering of gunfire. After that a massed wildness of sound. Thudding guns, bawling cattle, men's high crying.

He tried to get down the ridge fast enough to do something, but that smash to the side of the head hadn't done him a bit of good. The pulse of effort beat stronger and stronger until it was wild thunder in his head and his eyes began playing him tricks. He ran right through trees he thought were there and was knocked flat by impact with one he didn't see. He lay limply in a spinning, crazy world he couldn't get hold of.

He must have gone completely out for a time, for when he finally began to find coherence of mind and sense again, there was no conflict anywhere close to him. It was below, away, away below, with only an occasional shot and an occasional yell and the ever fading rumble and crash of cattle racing back along the way they had come.

It was clear enough now what had happened. Abel Hendron had won his round and won it decisively. The plains herd had been blocked, turned, and stampeded back down Kingfisher. That herd would be scattered far and wide before it quit running. It would take weeks of hard riding to get it together again. And what of the men who had been bringing in that herd—how had they come out of this? Dusty Elliot had been down there and Brace Shotwell and all the others. . . .

Kerchival started on down the ridge, more slowly now. Something was wet on the side of his head, and, when he put a hand up there, it came away sticky and stained with crimson. He was lucky that smash into the tree hadn't caved his skull in completely. A hard and ferocious ache had settled behind his eyes now and every jolting stride stirred it up.

Frustration gnawed at him. He had done no good for himself or anyone else. He had made his vows, spoken his brags, and when the chips were down had turned up useless. This thing should have been foreseen and adequately guarded against. The unease that had finally sent him on the abortive scout up ahead should have been heeded more quickly and the whole deal handled differently. . . .

He shook his tortured head. What might have been, hadn't been. There was no percentage in casting back. The present and the future had to be faced and handled. The first thing for him to do was to get back to headquarters and get another horse under him again. After that. . . .

He ducked for a handy tree, drew himself, tall and still, behind it, peering with bloodshot eyes down the shadowed slope below. Movement down there. Riders. Three of them, slipping through the timber, circling and climbing. The Ballards, coming back. For what?

Only one answer to that. For him. They had certainly seen his horse go down. Chances were one of them had fired the shot that had dropped his horse. So they would know he was afoot, miles from headquarters, and they meant to make the day one of complete victory by rounding him up.

Abel Hendron would have figured this out. He would have spread his other men across the lower slopes above Lazy Y to block the trails there, while the Ballards had come back to start the hunt for him from here, where he'd been unhorsed. Abel Hendron was shooting for high stakes this day, and so far had shot too well.

The Ballards were coming right up this ridge, almost as though they knew exactly where to look for him. He couldn't stay where he was. They had ridden past him once when he'd had scant cover, but that was when they had other things in mind—the turning and stampeding of the herd. Now it would be different. They were looking for him and him alone. . . .

The west slope of the ridge was the most thickly grown. In fact, some thirty yards below the crest there were jack pines. If he could get into the middle of them. . . .

He crouched, getting the bulk of the ridge point between him and the Ballards, and he went down the west slope at a run. He got into the jack pine thicket just before the upclimbing riders and horses lifted onto the ridge crest. They were close enough for him to hear the carry of their voices.

"This is the ridge, Spence," Gard Ballard said. "You dropped his horse right at the head of it. Maybe the fall busted him up. Turk, you go on up and see. If it didn't, he can't be too far from here."

Gard and Spence reined in. Turk spurred on up the ridge. The marks of Virg Hendron's fists still showed on his face, and memory of that beating had left Turk darkly sullen and vengeful. He was hungry for something to hit at. He carried his rifle across his saddle, ready for instant use.

When Turk vanished upridge, Gard dropped back in his saddle, relaxed, building a cigarette. But Spence, the venomous one, was alert, his hard eyes constantly swinging.

"I don't know yet how I missed him and got his horse," he grated. "Must have been the slope and the way the light came in from the side on my sights. If I'd just put that slug into him, this would have been a complete day."

"We'll get him," prophesied Gard complacently. "And we got him cut down to size now. That plains crowd got a bellyful this trip. I counted three of them down when they tried to hold the point, and the cattle must have caught more, runnin' over the drag. This time Hendron called the right turn."

"We got nothin' sure until we get Kerchival," said Spence harshly. "And that damned will. Hendron ain't got it. Who has? I think Hendron knows, but he clams up when you start talkin' about it." A thought seemed to strike Spence. "Maybe he has got the will . . . maybe he ain't showin' all his cards, even to us. Maybe his long-term idea is to push us out of the picture, too . . . after he's used us."

Gard laughed sardonically. "Don't tell me you've come to mistrust our estimable uncle, Spence."

Spence cursed. "I trust nobody but you and myself. Not even Turk. There's a streak in Turk. He tries to play it tough, but after seein' him quit to that damned Virg Hendron, I ain't bettin' a dime on him."

Gard stirred restlessly in his saddle. "We'll come out all right, you and Turk and me. We can drop Abel Hendron flat on his back if he tries to go phony on us. We'll get our half of everything, don't worry about that. Hendron can't get anywhere without us and he damn' well knows it."

"That's true enough," conceded Spence. "But just how much is he goin' to want from now on? Maybe not as much as he did once. Maybe he'll curl up and quit on us. He ain't the same man he was. Somethin's workin' in him. I think it's because of that fool girl, Lear. Her walkin' out on him didn't do him a bit of good. He ain't been the same since. Oh, he figgered this deal today and stood to it in good shape. But you never know, when things are workin' in a man like they are in him, when he'll cave. Virg goin' proud on him ain't helpin' matters, either. So I ain't bein' sure of anything until I see it happen with my own eyes or until I got it in my hand."

Turk came spurring back down the ridge. He held a broken rifle stock in his hand. "This is all I could find besides his horse," Turk reported. "Wherever he is, all he's got is a six-gun. What now?"

Gard took a last deep inhalation from his cigarette, crushed the butt on his saddle horn. "Let's see if we can figger which way he'd probably head. Not east, for that's War Hatchet range and he'd want no part of that. Not over Mount Cherokee, for he's afoot. But west, maybe, and then down, tryin' to come in on Lazy Y again. So we got Shacks and the others holdin' the trails around Lazy Y. We'll drift west a piece, then spread out and comb things between here and Lazy Y."

They were in plain view of Dave Kerchival, close enough so that he could see the expressions on their faces. And now, as they moved to Gard's plan of action, they swung to ride down and past his hiding place within short yards of him. He hugged the forest-matted earth.

It was Spence who made the discovery. Spence the doubter, the distrustful, the bitter, malevolent one. For, as he started his mount down the side of the ridge, Spence's glance flickered and settled on the marks Kerchival's boot heels had gouged in the soft slope in heading for the thicket below.

"Watch it!" yelled Spence. "Somebody came this way!"

Spence was high in his saddle, peering into the thicket. He cursed, whipped up his rifle, and shot, all in one slashing move. Again the drop of the slope fooled him. Dave Kerchival felt the bullet stir the shirt across his shoulders as it passed. This was it!

He shoved his gun ahead of him and began to shoot. His target was half clear, half blurred—man and horse whirling wildly as Spence tried to spur to the side while levering in another shell. Kerchival knew he had missed twice, but now Spence was ready to shoot again, rifle whipping up.

Kerchival had Spence's head and shoulders fairly clear. He tried for the center of this target and he saw the smash of the heavy bullet knock Spence back across the cantle of his saddle, where he hung, limpness beginning to soften him. His horse, spooked and wild from the sudden gunfire and the savage bite of Spence's spurs, spun on scrambling hoofs, and the motion flung Spence from the saddle in a spinning, rolling fall. In tumbled slackness Spence brought up against a pine sapling and never moved after that.

A rifle slug cut a small sapling completely in half, not a foot from Kerchival's face. Another slashed into the earth no farther away and flung up a gout of débris that stung Kerchival's taut cheeks and filled his eyes with blur. Off to the right, Turk Ballard was yelling incoherently and levering lead madly. Kerchival gave it back to him until his gun clicked empty.

He was only partially aware that Turk had quit shooting, that Turk's horse was spooking away, carrying a rider who had dropped his rifle and who was humped in the saddle, numbed by the agony of a bullet-shattered right arm. Kerchival was wondering about Gard who, cooler and more methodical than the others, would be pulling down carefully to make certain of his first shot.

Instinctively Kerchival was clawing at the loops of his belt, thumbing fresh cartridges free, trying to reload. But all the time he knew he'd never be in time. Gard—where was Gard Ballard?

He saw him then, standing in his stirrups, higher up the slope. He looked into Gard's eyes right over the ominous blue muzzle of Gard's rifle. The weapon was steady, dead on. It was like Gard, thought Kerchival, to make dead sure. He tensed himself to take the shock of the lead. . . .

Below and behind him a rifle crashed thinly. The bullet from it knocked Gard Ballard out of his saddle as though struck by some massive club. Dave Kerchival found himself clinging to a jack pine for support, panting as though from terrific physical effort. That shot that had saved his life? It must have been Dusty—good old Dusty Elliot, come up in the nick of time. Staggering a little, Kerchival pushed his way out of the lower side of the thicket, mumbling Dusty's name.

It wasn't Dusty. It was a pudgy little man with gray whisker stubble across his face—a frowsy-looking figure under a floppy brimmed hat. It was Jack Tully.

And Jack Tully had his rifle at his shoulder again, the muzzle steady and menacing on Kerchival's chest.

"Don't misunderstand my play, Dave," said Tully. "There's

more than one angle to this game. I take it that gun of yours is empty. Just the same . . . drop it!"

The tone was soft, almost amiable, but the look in Tully's eyes was a dead gray evil. Kerchival stared at the man, knowing a dazed bewilderment.

"I don't get this," he mumbled. "You downed Gard Ballard. You saved my life. Now . . . ?"

"Yeah," cut in Tully, "I downed him. Not for your sake, but for my own. That's the way I always play the game . . . for myself. Dave, I told you to drop that gun!"

Kerchival drew several long deep breaths, steadying himself. The strain, the fierce, draining activity of the past few minutes in which he had fought to live, in which he had had to kill or be killed, the building up of stark, raw emotion, had set his head to pounding again. There was anger in him, too, a craggy rage.

He squared himself, spread his feet. "No, by God!" he blurted harshly. "I won't!"

All the time Jack Tully had been edging in on him. Now, snake-fast, this deceptive, pudgy man moved. A slithering, long stride put him close enough and the barrel of his rifle whipped in a short, chopping arc. Kerchival threw up an arm that only partially warded off the blow. Enough of it was left to get through, and again thunder and agony racked his head. He went down into chaotic blackness.

Jack Tully stood over him, small, pursed lips pulled to a snarl. "You stubborn fool! Do you think I give a damn for you, outside of what you can bring me?"

CHAPTER SEVENTEEN

High up in the late afternoon gloom under the massive overhang of the Mount Cherokee rim, Dave Kerchival lay, conscious but with his eyes closed. His wrists were pulled behind him and tightly tied. His ankles were likewise bound. Another length of rope, threaded through the bonds about his wrists, reached out and was tied to the short, solid trunk of a tough and twisted aspen.

At the moment Kerchival was not trying to think; it was enough that he could lie utterly motionless so that the torment in his head could subside somewhat. This was Jack Tully's hide-out camp and right now Kerchival had it to himself. Tully had climbed up to his look-out and was watching all the spread of country below.

In time Kerchival stirred slightly, easing his position. He had taken two savage belts on the head, the impact against the tree when his horse had been shot out from under him, and then the clout from Jack Tully's rifle barrel. But these were beginning to wear off, the confused, fuzzy roaring in his ears had ceased, and, though his head ached murderously, channels of thought were clearing.

He had come up to this place from the spot where the shoot-out with the Ballards had taken place, jackknifed across a saddle. Tully had loaded him across that saddle somehow. Kerchival did not remember that part of it, but enough consciousness had returned by the time they arrived here for Kerchival to remember being hauled out of that saddle, dragged over to this spot, and then tied hand and foot. Since then he had just lain quietly, letting the dark shadows push fully back. And now thought was beginning to work once more.

It was pretty confusing to try and figure this thing. What was Jack Tully's part in it? Why had Tully shot Gard Ballard to save Dave Kerchival's life, and then tied him up and held him as a prisoner? Nothing added up except that he was alive. He had to be content with that for a while.

He heard the clump and crunch of boots as Jack Tully came back into camp. He still lay with closed eyes. Then he gasped and caught his breath as Tully sluiced his head and shoulders with half a bucket of icy spring water. After the first impact he was almost grateful, for the effect on his head was all to the good. He blinked against the moisture and looked up at Tully.

"You play a strange game, Jack," he said across stiff lips. "I suppose there's an answer?"

"There's an answer," Tully growled. "But whichever way the cat jumps, there'll be no comfort in it for you. At an offhand guess, just how much would you rate yourself worth . . . on the hoof?"

"I don't know what you're driving at . . . unless it's how much I'll pay for you to turn me loose."

Tully laughed sardonically. "It's not how much you'll pay. The paying will be done by somebody else. Well, sweet dreams."

Tully bent and looked over Kerchival's bonds, tested them, and was satisfied. Without another word he moved down to where his horse stood, still under saddle, took up a notch on the latigo, swung up, and rode off.

Dave Kerchival listened to the fading clack and shuffle of hoofs and presently all sound of them was gone and the weight of complete silence held this wild, lonely rim country. Kerchival was alone with nothing but his thoughts.

163

But these thoughts were alive now with ever quickening alertness. Jack Tully's last remarks had been in the nature of a shade jerked aside, opening a corridor of brand-new conjecture, and along that corridor events that had been up to now blind alleys of thwarted reasoning fell into logical sequence.

Step by step Dave Kerchival took his thinking along that sequence and something cold and savage came up inside him as all the answers lined up. He began a fight against his bonds, writhing and twisting and straining, then knew a sudden helplessness and dismay. No hope here. Jack Tully had set those bonds to stay.

Kerchival considered the proposition of setting up a yell, discarded it immediately. That would be like the chirping of a single cricket against all the vastness of the universe.

Kerchival twisted around on his side until he could look over the frugal set-up of this camp. Tully intended a return, of course, and his gear was scattered around. There was the untidy heap of his blankets and there the blackened small area where his fire had burned with a few smoked-up cooking utensils stacked beside it. There was a small log with a short-handled axe stuck into it where Tully had chopped his firewood.

Kerchival wondered about those dead fire ashes. Maybe, deep in their depths, there might still linger a live coal. If he could roll to that spot and get a coal against the thongs about his wrist. . . . He tried it and was brought up short by the rope that was threaded through his wrist bonds and then tied to the aspen trunk. Jack Tully had been smart. Kerchival wasn't rolling anywhere. He was like a tethered animal. At farthest reach he still lacked a couple of yards of reaching the fire area.

Shadows were deepening under the Mount Cherokee rim; the afternoon was beginning to run out fast. In another hour—dusk. And after that—swift dark. After that—what?

Kerchival began fighting his bonds again. The answers that

he and Joe Orchard had searched for so fruitlessly before—well, now he had them all and was helpless to do anything about them. The frustration of this made him grind his teeth, and he strained at his bonds until he was drenched with sweat and numbness crept over him and his head took on a savage beating once more. And all to no use. He couldn't gain the slightest fraction of slack. He went limp again, panting thickly from his exertions.

He took another look around, propped slightly up on hands and wrists that felt like useless clubs. And suddenly his lips peeled back and a gleam of desperate hope lighted his eyes. Had Jack Tully been quite as smart as he thought? Had this cold, sly, pudgy man, so crassly deadly, forgotten that a short length of rope plus the length of a tall man's legs . . . ?

Dave Kerchival writhed his way out to the farthest stretch of that tethering rope, rolled over almost on his face, reached out with his feet. He had to twist his head at a hard angle to see. That axe, sticking in the chopping log—it was still a good foot beyond the reach of his feet. Well—how far back could he bend his arms?

He used the hunched pressure of a shoulder against the earth, forcing his body out and out. The pull of the tethering rope began to drag his arms back until the muscles about his chest and shoulders were taut with strain. His reaching feet touched the chopping log. He needed a little more distance and he burrowed against the earth until needles of pain jabbed through his tortured arms. He couldn't twist his head enough to see any more; he would have to work blind now, and by feel.

He bent his knees, lifting his bound feet upward, felt the touch of the axe handle. He had to hook his toes over that. But if, in the try, he kicked the axe loose and it fell on the far side of the log, then he was done for. Gritting his teeth, face ground against the earth, sweat oozing all over him, he strained a little closer. He thought the pull of the rope would disjoint his arms completely. He bent his knees once more, straightened them with a hooking lunge. His toes hooked across the axe handle and the down-pulling weight of his legs turned the chopping log—toward him!

He relaxed, panting in gusty gulps. He'd done it! The rest was just a matter of time. He was able to let up some on the strain on his arms and still reach the axe with his feet. The axe was set pretty solidly in the chopping log, but his nudging feet finally kicked it free. Then, his boot toes furrowing the earth, he began working it toward him. At first it was agonizingly slow, but gradually he gained ground. It was a case of move the axe a little, then gouge his boot heels into the ground and push his body back.

The strain on his arms lessened. Bit by bit he worked the axe along the ground toward the aspen trunk that held him prisoner. And finally it was done. He had the axe close enough so that he could roll upon it and feel the cold metal against his bound hands, could even grip it partially with his stiffened fingers.

He sat up, twisted the axe head so its cutting edge was up, held it that way with the weight of his body on the handle. Then, fumbling until he had the axe's keen edge between his wrists and against the bonds, he began rubbing these back and forth, bearing down with all the weight he could.

It was not only bonds that he cut. Again and again he could feel the slide of steel across his wrists and the slime of blood begin to seep. But he kept at it blindly, doggedly, until abruptly there was no more tension and his hands were free.

He swung them around in front of him, stared at them through a mist of sweat. They were swollen, blood-smeared— but free. They felt like clubs as he went to work on the knots of the rope that held his ankles together and there seemed to be no strength at all in his fingers. He beat his hands against the earth to speed up circulation and it came with the prickling of a thousand needles. And so, after another interval of dogged struggle, his feet were free.

He got to his feet and staggered about drunkenly. It was like trying to walk on stumps. But this didn't matter and neither did the nagging throb in his beaten head, for a strong tide of exultation bore him up. He was free.

He had no gun; he had no horse. But once more he was his own man. He stumbled through the fringe of brush that walled this hide-out camp below the rim and he saw the far slope falling away beneath him, still and empty and smoking up with the blue shadows of dusk.

The sun had gone and the chill of the high country came washing in. It felt good against his face and throat and was high wine in his lungs. He went lurching down the slope, hair and head scabbed with dried blood, lines carved deeply in his face. But there was a cold flame in his eyes. He was a tall man, and lean, and vengeance-bound.

CHAPTER EIGHTEEN

On a low point where the timber thinned and laid long, still corridors on either hand, Abel Hendron sat his horse and waited out the dragging hours. He had men spread out across the slope, watching and waiting just as he was. Abel Hendron's face was a gray, set mask and he was a stiff and unrelenting figure in the saddle. But there was no luster in his eyes and he had the look somehow of a man surveying a triumph that was mocking and empty.

So far this day had gone exactly according to plan. With the full weight of his entire force behind him, he had stopped the plains herd, had turned it and sent it hurtling back along the way it had come. It had been a savage stroke, timed to perfection, and working out to that same perfection.

It had cost the lives of men; point riders of the herd had been overwhelmed, shot out of their saddles. Men in the drag of the herd could have escaped the thundering deluge only by the wildest sort of riding, and some there may have been caught and rolled under. When and where the cattle had stopped running was any man's guess, but of one thing there could be no doubt—it would take much riding and time to get that herd together again and much resolution and planning before another attempt to move it up past the Mount Cherokee rim would be made. And this attempt might very well never be made if a final all-important item could be closed out. That item was Dave Kerchival.

Abel Hendron had seen Kerchival's horse shot out from under him. He would have given much to have stopped at the time and made sure of Kerchival, but to have done that might have upset the advantage of surprise in charging the herd and so bungled that operation completely. And it was all-important that the herd be stopped and turned.

That had been done, and now the problem was to get Kerchival. For it was Abel Hendron's judgment that such men as Brace Shotwell and Joe Kirby, if they still lived, would be too thoroughly dismayed and discouraged after this setback ever to try another drive to the high summer range. Particularly would this be so if Dave Kerchival did not survive to lead another attempt.

The Ballards, knowing this country better than the outside riders Hendron had brought in, had ridden up to comb the higher slope, to locate the spot where Kerchival's horse had gone down and to pick up the trail from there. If still able to travel, Kerchival would, reasoned Hendron, try to get back to Lazy Y headquarters, and it was Hendron's plan to block him off and trap him. So far there had been no sign of the quarry, and no report from the Ballards, either.

A rider came pushing up from the timber below. It was the tough outside rider, Shacks. He reported his mission profanely.

"There's some holed up at Lazy Y, meanin' business and takin' no chances. I crept up as close as I could to look things over an' damn' near got my hair parted." Shacks took off his hat and fingered a bullet slash in the crown.

Abel Hendron nodded brusquely. "They'll keep. All else will be easy, once we get Kerchival."

"One of the boys said he thought he heard some shootin', high up, a while back," said Shacks. "Hard to tell just where or how far away. Big country up there, an' timber makes echoes do funny things. No word from the Ballards yet?"

"Nothing. We'll hold this line and wait. If we don't turn Kerchival up by dark, then we've lost him."

Well out to the right a shout echoed faintly. Shacks whipped around in his saddle, stared that way. "Well, now. . . ."

They waited, watching and listening, and soon a rider came spurring along the slope. It was one of Hendron's new and wild crew. Shacks said: "Dobe Higgins. Somethin's happened!"

Higgins set his horse up with a rush, looking at Hendron. "You're wanted yonder. The Ballards run into somethin'. The young one, Turk, is back yonder with a smashed-up arm. He's scared green an' moanin' somethin' about Spence an' Gard bein' dead."

A ripple of movement went through Abel Hendron, pulling him even straighter in the saddle. Gray shadow blotted all expression from his eyes. He spun his horse, lifted it to a run.

Turk Ballard was flat on his back, another of the outside riders wrapping a sweat-stained neckerchief about the crippled arm. Turk was whimpering and moaning. Abel Hendron swung from his saddle, dropped on one knee beside Turk.

"Tell me," he said harshly. "What happened?"

If there had ever been any toughness in Turk Ballard, there was none left now. He stared up at Hendron wildly.

"Kerchival," he whimpered. "We stumbled into him. Spence . . . he got Spence. He smashed my arm. Gard . . . I'm not sure about Gard. But there was somebody else I didn't see, who bought in. And I figger Gard musta got it, too."

"You never stopped to find out, of course," said Shacks with hard contempt. "You were winged and you run for it. You yellow. . . ."

Abel Hendron swung his head. "That will do! Help me get him on his horse again."

They boosted Turk into his saddle. Hendron looked up the still and mocking slope. "Get the rest of the men, Shacks, and see if you can backtrack Turk to where . . . where . . . it happened. Bring in what you find to War Hatchet."

"What about Kerchival?" asked Shacks.

"Too late, there," said Hendron woodenly. "Forget Kerchival unless you should chance to meet up with him. In that case, you know what to do."

It was a long, slow ride back to War Hatchet. By the time he got there, Abel Hendron had to hold Turk Ballard in the saddle. At War Hatchet there was Joe Orchard, talking with Deaf Blair, who was deaf in one ear only and could hear very well indeed with the other. They helped Hendron get Turk Ballard out of his saddle and into the bunkhouse. Then Joe Orchard faced Abel Hendron grimly.

"Range wars are something I can't do much about, Hendron," said Joe harshly. "But murder is something else. As yet I ain't got a thing on you, but the trails I've been smoking out keep pointing more and more in one direction. Once I'm sure, I'm coming for you. You've got a lot to answer for, more than I'd care to have on my conscience. It's my fancy that I see the shadows of Bill Yeager and Mel Rhodes behind your shoulder, Hendron."

Abel Hendron did not seem to hear him as he looked at Deaf Blair. "Saddle up, Blair . . . and go to town after Doctor Cable."

Joe Orchard had no respect for Turk Ballard, but he was a humane man. "I've seen men shot through the middle make less fuss than him," he growled. "But I'll go get Doc Cable. First . . . who got lead into Turk?"

"Your friend," said Hendron thinly. "Kerchival."

Joe Orchard headed for his horse and across his shoulder he said: "Good man, Dave Kerchival. He don't whip easy. He'll live for a long time."

A heavy slug of whiskey quieted Turk down. Hendron went out, unsaddled both his own and Turk's horse, and turned the animals into the cavvy corral. He moved slowly and methodically. He still carried himself tautly straight, but his usually expressionless face reflected a stunned apathy. Over and over he seemed to hear Turk's jerky words: *Spence is done for. Gard . . . I don't know about Gard. . . .*

He went over to his office in the ranch house. It and all the rest of the house were full of empty gloom. Lear wasn't there; Virg wasn't there. Nobody was there but himself. It was his castle, but it was empty of everything but pointing shadows. He walked through it, from room to room, listening for sounds where there was none. Lear's soft, quick steps—where were they?

For how many years had he been a madman, driven by ambitions without limit and seeking any means to fulfill them? Blind pride, unlimited egotism, and selfish purpose. These he had fed upon and used as guiding lines in his life. And somewhere along the way he'd sold out to the devil completely. He went back to his office and sat there, a man withering up and dying inside.

The raw, savage events of this day seemed suddenly far away and of no moment. The scattering of the plains herd—where had he profited by that? Turk Ballard—out in the bunkhouse with a bullet-shattered arm. Spence and Gard dead—yes, somehow he was sure they were dead. And Lear and Virg gone, moved out of his life, because in him, their own father, they had seen things they could no longer live with or excuse. It was as though a keen-edged knife had dropped, cutting clean through the whole fabric of his existence, leaving him with much, and with nothing—nothing at all.

He was not surprised when, through the first shadows of sunset, Shacks and the others rode in, bringing two dead men across saddles. Spence and Gard Ballard, of course. Somehow he'd known what they would find up there along the Kingfisher trail. Two still figures to emphasize the grim tally and to mock him with the emptiness of his conquest for power and gain. He did not go out, but waited for Shacks to report at the office.

Shacks said: "No trace of Kerchival. Slippery *hombre* and a tough one, that feller. We'll hear from him again."

"I will," droned Abel Hendron tonelessly. "You won't. You will put Gard and Spence in the saddle shed and cover them with blankets. Then you will get your gear together and come over here for your time. I'm paying you off . . . all of you."

Shacks stared at him, amazed. "You quittin' now, Hendron? Hell, man . . . now's when we got them on the run. Kerchival, me and the boys will take care of him. So you lost two in Gard and Spence Ballard. Well, I can round up a dozen tough ones to take their place. In ten days you'll own this range as far as you want to ride."

Abel Hendron was already reaching for his time book and checkbook. "You will do as I say. I'll have your time ready in half an hour."

"What the devil!" sputtered Shacks. "I don't understand. . . ."

"No," cut in Abel Hendron, "you don't. Neither did I, fully, until today . . . until just a little while ago. . . ." He shook his head as though to wring mocking, haunting thoughts from it, and now some of his old imperious harshness came back. "That will be all, Shacks."

The checks were ready when Shacks came for them, and Hendron stayed at his desk, listening to the thump of hoofs fade out and die in the thickening dusk.

It was early dark when Dr. Cable came spurring in and Hendron stepped out to greet him. Dr. Cable could be a brusque man when he wanted to, and he was brusque now.

"I'm here, Hendron, not because I want to be, but because the oath of my profession is a serious thing with me. I've neither liking nor respect for you or any of the Ballards, but professionally that is beside the point. Where is he?"

Hendron led the way to the bunkhouse. Dr. Cable made a swift examination, then began to roll up his sleeves. "I think I can save the arm," he said. "But I won't guarantee it will ever be straight again. Stick around. I may need help."

CHAPTER NINETEEN

There was a timbered ridge that ran out and dropped off abruptly in a blunt point above the meadow in which War Hatchet headquarters stood. Crouched in hiding on that ridge point, Jack Tully watched a flow of events take place below him. He had reached this spot just in time to see Shacks and the others ride in with the bodies of Gard and Spence Ballard and he wondered how they had happened to find these so soon.

Through the growing dusk he watched Shacks and the other outside riders carry war bags from the bunkhouse and tie these to their saddles, and, when he saw them ride away from War Hatchet, he knew by these signs that the riders were leaving for good. And this was something else to startle him and make him wonder. Had something happened to Abel Hendron? In that headlong charge that Hendron had led to turn and stampede the plains herd, had Hendron stopped a slug? Was this the reason for what seemed the breaking up of War Hatchet?

No, that wasn't the answer. Hendron must be down there, in his office where yellow lamplight now glowed, unless Virg had taken over. But this was unlikely, for Virg Hendron, as Jack Tully knew him, was not the sort to act with any such swift decision if responsibility were tossed into his lap.

Tully wondered how many were down there at the headquarters. Well, he'd make sure of that when he went in. There was no hurry about this thing now. For he held all the high cards. Hendron would have to deal his way.

With full dark, Tully began moving in closer to the ranch buildings. He was crouched at a corner of the corrals when Dr. Cable rode in. Against the light shining from the bunkhouse door he identified Dr. Cable and Abel Hendron and Deaf Blair as they went in. He saw Deaf Blair come out and go over to the cook shack several times, carrying back pails of hot water. It was a watch that dragged on for a full hour before Dr. Cable finally rode away. And after that the taut, straight figure of Abel Hendron was momentarily limned against the light of the office door before he went in and closed the door behind him.

Jack Tully straightened up and crossed to that door quickly. He knew all he wanted to know now. Aside from whoever it was that lay wounded in the bunkhouse, War Hatchet was deserted except for Hendron and Deaf Blair, and about old Deaf, Tully had small concern.

With a single move Tully opened the office door and stepped inside. He had a gun in his free hand. "Now watch yourself, Hendron," he rapped. "We got to have a talk, you and me. We got things to settle. Watch it, I say!"

Abel Hendron had just seated himself at his desk again. Now he made no move except to tip his head and stare. Then he shrugged and said: "Why not? This seems to be the kind of a day when many things are being settled."

Over in the bunkhouse Deaf Blair was a troubled man. For long years he'd been cook at War Hatchet. He had never understood Abel Hendron, the man for whom he worked, and had never bothered to try. There had been things about War Hatchet that Deaf hadn't liked, and others that he had. He'd always been fond of Lear Hendron and of Virg, too. To crusty old Deaf, who had no kin of his own, they were like his own kids. He'd made allowance for Virg's orneriness, figuring that someday Virg would snap out of it and grow up. And the morning that Virg had whipped sheer hell out of Turk Ballard, right in Deaf's own cook shack, Deaf knew that moment had arrived and that Virg would pan out all right after all.

But these things could not make up for all the other bitter things that had taken place. The old crew, with Dave Kerchival as foreman, were long gone, driven off by Abel Hendron's ever increasing harsh autocracy. Lear had left and then Virg. Now there was conflict and death, with two of the Ballards laid out in the saddle shed and with Turk, here, with a badly shot-up arm.

Deaf looked along the bunkhouse at Turk, who lay deeply still under an opiate. The bunkhouse smelled strongly of iodoform. Deaf had never liked Turk Ballard, or his brothers, either, for that matter. But he didn't consider that now. What Deaf was thinking was that whatever fell within the circle of Abel Hendron's power and influence was either destroyed or driven off. Deaf had been growing increasingly restless, particularly since Lear had gone to town to live. And it came to Deaf now that he, too, must move on. He didn't know where he'd go, but he had a few dollars saved up. And it was time to quit. For there was nothing left at War Hatchet for him, it seemed. And as long as his mind was made up, he might as well go tell Abel Hendron about it now.

Deaf started for the bunkhouse door and got there just in time to see a man open the door of Abel Hendron's office and dodge swiftly in. In the brief glow of lamplight Deaf saw something flash in the man's hand. It could be nothing else but a gun.

Deaf went on up to the office door, but he went with caution, and, when he got there, he flattened his good ear against the door and listened.

Abel Hendron was just saying: "I told you the other day I wouldn't pay through the nose for that will, Tully. I'm not interested now. I'm not interested in anything you may bring me."

"Well, now . . . I wouldn't be too sure of that, Hendron," mocked Tully. "Suppose I told you I could bring you Dave Kerchival's scalp. How much would that be worth to you?"

"Nothing. Even that wouldn't interest me now. You've killed him?"

Tully laughed. "So you are interested, after all. No, he's alive. But I got him where I can produce him. Let's come down to hard facts, Hendron. You want Lazy Y. You've always wanted it. Well, I took care of Bill Yeager for you. You paid pretty good for *that*. Then I got hold of Yeager's will, which left everything to Dave Kerchival. You bluffed around, saying that will didn't mean anything, anyhow. But you knew better. You knew that, if that will got back into Kerchival's hands, you were blocked away from Lazy Y more completely than ever. Even if we got Kerchival, unless we had the will, too, you still couldn't grab Lazy Y and be sure of holding it, for the courts could move in then. In other words, the will without Kerchival wasn't any good to us, and Kerchival without the will was the same. So you said when I offered you the will the other day. But things are different now. Right now I can offer you both the will and Kerchival. That's what you want, ain't it?"

"When you said things were different now, you were more than right," said Abel Hendron stonily. "They are . . . very much. I say again that I'm not interested in anything you might bring me . . . anything. Understand?"

"No," answered Tully bluntly, "I don't. You're not the sort to quit trying to grab as long as there's anything to grab. And don't try and pull a noble or holy pose on me. I've known you too well and for too long. Clear back to when we rode cavalry trails together. When you were the rising young officer and I was just plain Jack Tully, supply sergeant. Made money in those days, didn't we, Hendron . . . with you requisitioning the stuff and me selling it. Split some pretty good chunks between us, we did. And got out of the service just ahead of an investigation that didn't quite come off. Thieves we were, Hendron . . . and still are. Only you're proud, while I'm not. Now let's get down to cases and quit this fancy dancing around. I got the will and I got Kerchival. How much for both?"

Abel Hendron's face was a mask, but it was a gray and lifeless one. Only his hard brown eyes seemed alive and they were sick. He spoke through stiff lips: "In the last few hours I've taken the first clear look at myself in years, Tully. What I've seen is something no decent man could stomach. Yet I'm still a long way above you. For pay you dry-gulched Bill Yeager. You knifed Mel Rhodes to get that will. I still don't understand why you didn't kill Kerchival instead of just gun-whipping him, when you thought he had the will on him. What held you back then?"

Again Tully laughed and there was rising evil in the sound. "Because I didn't trust you, my fine-feathered friend. I needed Kerchival alive as a club over you . . . to make you come across. I still got him alive and he's still a club. And don't try and strut on me. If I killed for pay, you paid for the killing. If that makes you a better man than me, I don't see it. Wonder what your girl would think if she knew these things? Mebbe even that whelp, Virg, might gag over them."

Abel Hendron reared up in his chair. "Keep your tongue off my girl and boy, Tully." Hendron's voice rang hoarsely. "Leave them out of this."

Jack Tully's eyes pinched down, glittering with a sardonic light. "You've just given me a wonderful idea, Hendron. You say you're not interested in paying for the will, or for Kerchival. But how much will you pay to make sure all the sweet truth about you doesn't get to the ears of Lear and Virg? How much, Hendron?"

Something ran completely out of Abel Hendron. He seemed to shrink, to shrivel. "You wouldn't . . . do that?" It was almost a groan.

"Ah," said Tully softly, "now wouldn't I? Afraid you don't know me as well as I know you, Hendron. There's no soft spot in me. I let you live the other day after you tried to throw a gun on me, not because I loved you, my friend, but because you represent profit to me. It'll be big profit this time, for the price will be high. Every red cent you can beg, borrow, or steal, unless you want the truth to reach those beloved ears. Should be quite a chunk of money, Hendron."

Hendron slid down in his chair. "That," he mumbled jerkily, "does put the price high, Tully."

The sudden drop in his right shoulder betrayed him. Abel Hendron never had been a fast man with a gun. Now, as he tried to draw and get Tully across the desk, he was no match for this pudgy, deadly man's deceptive speed. And Tully did not hold back this time, for he rightly read the gray desperation in Abel Hendron's face. This time Hendron was going all the way. So, just as the muzzle of Hendron's gun cleared the edge of the desk, Tully shot him, twice.

Abel Hendron lunged forward against the desk, then crumpled back, wilting in his chair.

Outside, Deaf Blair yelled, having no other weapon, then flung himself against the door. Snake-fast, Jack Tully snuffed the lamp and ducked through the door that led from the office to the rest of the ranch house. He could not be sure how many men were behind that yell. Maybe there'd been more of them in the bunkhouse than he thought. Maybe some had just ridden in. Maybe. . . .

Tully found his way through the house's blackness to a back door and darted off into the night. A lot of careful scheming had gone up in smoke, back there in that office. Tully cursed as he ran.

CHAPTER TWENTY

It was a long jaunt down the slope of Mount Cherokee for a man on foot. It was longer when he'd taken the physical punishment Dave Kerchival had. But Kerchival was a man driven by cold purpose now, and there were wells of natural strength that lay deep and vital in him. In the black dark he came within hailing distance of Lazy Y headquarters. There was no light about the place, but Kerchival could smell wood smoke. Somebody was about, but he could not be sure just who. Maybe it was Perk O'Dair and Chick Roland, holding fast to their trust, or maybe Hendron, with superior numbers, had rooted out the two young riders out and had taken over himself. There was only one way to find out, and, even if it were hostile forces, they would have little chance of locating him in this dark. Kerchival lifted a shout that was hoarse and a little ragged.

"Hello . . . the cabin! Anybody there?"

There was a slight pause before a reply came, in Perk O'Dair's voice.

"Who is it?"

"Kerchival, Perk. I'm coming in."

"Dave! Man . . . come on . . . come on! Hey, Chick . . . Dusty . . . it's Dave out there!"

They came to meet him, swearing their gruff relief. "Thought they had you, fellah," growled Dusty. "Thought they had you, sure. They had us forted up most of the day, then pulled out for some reason. I rode a circle just before dark, seein' if I could locate you. We aimed to really comb the slope, come daylight tomorrow. Man . . . this is good . . . good!"

They poured hot coffee spiked with whiskey into him. He lay on a bunk while Dusty doctored his head, washing it carefully with hot water, then fashioning a bandage. Then he sat up to the table and wolfed hot food, and the comfort of it soothed some of the lines from his face and sent new strength surging through him. While he ate, they told him about the cattle and the men who had driven them.

"Shotwell and Kirby lost three men who were riding point," said Dusty. "Joe Kirby got off lucky. He only picked up a broken leg. A bunch of runnin' cattle caught him, threw his horse. There was a down log that Joe was able to crawl behind. That's all that kept him from being trampled to rags. Shotwell and their crowd took Joe in to Warm Creek for care. They're pretty discouraged. We took a beating, Dave."

Kerchival nodded grimly. "So did they." And then he told about the Ballards and about his own experiences with Jack Tully. Perk and Chick gaped with amazement at this last, but Dusty swore savagely.

"That *hombre!* I never could figure him, but I never did trust him. What the devil kind of game is he up to, Dave?"

"A deep one, Dusty. He had Joe Orchard fooled, he had me fooled . . . up to this. He was right under our noses all the time, the answer to a lot of things. Now I'm going back up after him. One of you boys go tie a saddle on a good bronc' for me. And I'll want guns."

"Not tonight," objected Dusty. "You been through plenty, Dave. You got to get some rest. Tomorrow we'll all. . . ."

"No," cut in Kerchival harshly, "I'm going tonight. And we can't leave these headquarters unguarded. This game isn't played out yet. I know where that camp under the rim is. I'm getting back there and I've got no time to lose. I don't need any

183

rest. This grub . . . knowing you boys are all right . . . well, I'm fit to go. Chick, go saddle that bronc'!"

Chick went out. Perk O'Dair spoke slowly: "So the Ballards are done, eh?"

"Gard and Spence for sure." Kerchival nodded. "Turk broke and rode for it. But he was hit."

"Maybe that'll slow Abel Hendron up," said Perk, "when he realizes the cost can roll up on both sides. He's sure pushed this thing to a bloody mess. Question is, will he ever pay enough . . . personally?"

"It'll catch up with him," said Kerchival stonily. "It always does."

Ten minutes later Dave Kerchival was once more in the saddle, threading black timber aisles, his horse breasting Mount Cherokee's long slope. Under his knee was a rifle, on his hip rode a short gun. Ahead of him lay a trail from which there would be no turning back until one more grim tally was completed.

The horse was fresh, strong, and eager from long hours in the corral. Dave Kerchival did not hold it back, but let it fling its good strength into the labor of the climb. Time was a vital element here. There was no way of telling how long Jack Tully would be absent from his camp, for many things could influence that. Only one thing was certain. Tully would be back, and Kerchival was wondering if, now that a turn in his luck had come, the tricky jade of fortune would continue to smile on him. So much in life, he mused, could hinge on so little. In his case a cold and deadly schemer's oversight in leaving an axe stuck in a chopping log at a distance measured in almost precise inches. Had that log been even half a foot farther away, well. . . .

Kerchival shook himself. That part of it all was past. Coming up was something else, and now it was time that held the answer. If Jack Tully got back to his hide-out camp first, found the man he had so confidently left as a prisoner gone—then there would be a long and desperate chase ahead. For Tully, animal cunning would make him spook and ride far and fast. He'd know full well the vengeance that would be riding his trail. He would tangle his trail and lay it across wide distances. And he'd be watching over his shoulder while he rode, ready at any time to hole up and pull an ambush on whoever was following him.

Kerchival wished that Joe Orchard was riding with him. For this chore was rightly Joe's. Joe's and the law's. But there'd been no time to locate Joe and so it must be done this way. Kerchival drew on his mount's willingness and lifted it to a faster pace.

Stars were shining in the chilling heavens, their light raking the timber tops with pale silver. But down beneath the trees where Kerchival rode this light could not reach, and for the most part he had to allow his horse its head, let it weave its own way through the black timber aisles. As long as the way was steadily up, Kerchival had to be content.

He had forgotten all physical discomfort, living entirely in a mental sphere, his mind reaching ahead to that hide-out camp, wondering if he would find it empty, planning what he would do when he got there, whether ahead of Tully or behind him. He came back to concrete things when, abruptly, he found the timber thinning about him and ahead the starlit shale and brush country below the rim.

For the first time since leaving headquarters, he reined in. He stood in his stirrups, looking and listening. Up above, black and solid against the stars, curved the long run of the rim. Silence held absolute except for the peevish barking of a fox, distant to the point of being little more than the faintest of echoes, this and the cold, pure fluting of a night hawk, adrift on noiseless wings somewhere up among the stars.

Kerchival sent his horse ahead, angling up and to the west. Tully's approach would necessarily be from the eastern side, for on the east lay War Hatchet, and Kerchival did not want to run the risk of crossing trails. So little could warn Tully, start the long hunt.

Three quarters of the way across the brush belt Kerchival left his horse and went on afoot. Now he could no longer ignore the physical. Stiffness made his legs clumsy at first, but this wore off as he climbed. He had the hide-out camp located by the shape of the rim above it and he worked his way in for the last two hundred yards with all the stealth he could muster.

It was black in there, Stygian. Kerchival went the last few yards virtually on hands and knees, keening the night with senses drawn razor-sharp with strain and pressure. The camp lay utterly still and empty. Either Tully had come and gone, or he had not yet returned. There was one way to be fairly sure. Kerchival felt his way about, found the long-dead ashes of the fire with cooking gear beside it, and then put his hand on the tangle of Tully's blankets.

Cold exultation raced through Kerchival. He had beaten Tully back. For if Tully had returned and gone, he would have taken blankets and cooking gear along. Now to wait this thing out.

He selected a spot closer in against the rim's base and hunkered there on his heels, stoically setting himself to wait this whole night out if necessary. He put his rifle beside him, drew his belt gun, and laid it across his lap. The night's chill bit at him and he hunched his shoulders against it.

A smoke would have helped, but this was out of the question. On this moist night air the scent of tobacco smoke would be as warning as a shout to a man like Jack Tully.

The wait was shorter than he'd hoped for. Not a quarter of an hour after he'd settled himself, Kerchival caught the first sounds of approach, the slap of a horse's scrambling hoofs across a spread of shale.

Jack Tully came straight in, morose and savage over the way all his carefully laid plans had backfired and come to nothingness because of the impasse he had run into far down at War Hatchet headquarters. He had not read Abel Hendron's make-up as correctly as he thought, had never guessed that with complete victory right in his hands Hendron would suddenly break and begin to retreat.

Tully could not understand a man like that, because he saw all things by his own hard, vicious, unrelenting code. There was no softness in Jack Tully anywhere and he had thought Abel Hendron was another with the same make-up. Hendron's life had been guided for so long by that overweening lust to dominate and control, that it had seemed reasonable to believe that nothing would ever turn him from it. That he would haggle over the price asked for Bill Yeager's will and for Dave Kerchival's scalp, Tully had expected. But in the end he'd been sure Hendron would pay. And Hendron hadn't. Something had gone out of the man, suddenly. And then, when Tully had tried pressure from another angle, Hendron had gone for his gun and brought the whole scheme crashing down.

Now Tully had nothing. He'd gambled everything, and lost everything. On the way up from War Hatchet he'd played with the idea of trying to make a deal with Kerchival—a deal for Bill Yeager's will and for Kerchival's life. And he had to throw this thought away because he knew that in Kerchival he had a man who would never trade anything with him but hot lead, should he ever get the chance.

It was a chance Tully did not intend to let him have. For Tully knew what he had to do now—saw clearly the only out left to him. That was to kill Kerchival and then ride, far and fast, go on the dodge, find new pastures, and lose himself under the anonymity of a changed name.

His chances of doing this were good. There were a lot of tangled trails left down below that would take considerable straightening out before the law would know which way to work. As for Kerchival, it could be months before his fate would be known, if ever; this was big country and could hide much. By daylight Tully figured he could be far across Mount Cherokee, with a well-hidden trail behind him. No, he had little to fear there. But it did grind him to find himself with empty hands, where he thought he'd have them well filled with Abel Hendron's money.

Well, he'd get this thing over quick. No sense in talking or arguing or dragging it out. He'd go over to where Kerchival lay, gun him, then get his gear together and move out. He might cook up a pot of coffee first, though—for the night had turned bitterly cold.

He pushed his horse through the last aspen fringe, swung down, and walked over past the chopping log. "Well, Kerchival," he said, "Hendron wouldn't pay. So that's your hard luck. Can't keep you now, and I can't let you go. Nothing personal in this, you understand. Just a matter of business and necessity."

Tully drew his gun and the lock clicked as he pulled the hammer back. It was utterly black against the ground and Tully kicked out to locate Kerchival's body. His boot met nothing.

Tully froze, holding his breath, then letting it out in a single gusty challenge.

"Kerchival!"

From behind and above him, the reply came. "Over here, Jack. You shouldn't have left the axe so close."

Dave Kerchival had flattened himself close to the ground on first being certain of Tully's approach. In this blackness a man would have only two things to shoot at, sound or gun flame. Of the two, sound would be the trickiest target. Kerchival had to gamble on that. He had to give Tully first bite and hope that Tully would shoot high.

Tully did. He came around and his gun smashed twice, flame lancing, report blasting back from the rim wall in trapped and pounding echoes. And Kerchival's gamble paid off. No lead touched him and he had Tully marked by his flaming gun. He shot with cold intentness, once—twice—a third time.

He heard Tully go down. He heard him flounder, heard him gasp, heard the final breath run out of him in a long, whistling sigh. And then he waited for his eyes to come back to normal after the searing suddenness of the guns' crimson tongues. He had plenty of time to wait. There was no hurry now. This thing was done.

CHAPTER TWENTY-ONE

Gray dawn was breaking when Dave Kerchival again rode into Lazy Y headquarters, Jack Tully's horse following at lead, its owner tied across the saddle. Dusty Elliot came through the dim light to meet him, and Dusty's words were few while his relief was great.

"So you got him!"

"I beat him back to his camp." Kerchival nodded wearily. "And I beat him in the showdown. It's all even for Bill Yeager and Mel Rhodes now, Dusty."

"For Abel Hendron, too, Dave," Dusty said.

Kerchival, just swung from his saddle, jerked tall. "For Abel Hendron . . . what do you mean?"

"Hendron's dead, Dave. Tully killed him. Come on inside. Deaf Blair's got the story. Deaf came tearing in here about an hour after you left. Perk went to town after Joe Orchard and Joe's here now, too. We ought to straighten out a lot of things."

It was grim and quiet in the cabin. Chick Roland handed Kerchival a scalding cup of coffee, and Kerchival, cradling it between both hands, backed up to the stove and looked at Deaf Blair, who sat hunched on the end of a bunk.

"All right, Deaf," said Kerchival.

"I wasn't thinkin' very good or I might have stopped it," mumbled Deaf. "Hendron was in his office and I happened to see Tully duck in at the door. I went up to the door and listened and I heard a lot of things that sure had me fightin' my head, had me too smothered down to realize things were comin' to a boil. I heard Tully talk about how him and Hendron used to ride the cavalry together, how Hendron used to requisition stuff which Tully sold and then they split the profits. That was only part of it."

Deaf Blair held an empty coffee cup. Chick Roland filled it again and Deaf sipped noisily before going on.

"I don't recall exactly what each of 'em said, but the picture shapes up this way. Hendron paid Tully for dry-gulching Bill Yeager. But after that there was that will of Yeager's that still blocked things. So Tully set out to get hold of it and he knifed Mel Rhodes to do it."

Dusty Elliot said: "That ought to answer who it was that buffaloed you and went through your pockets right here in this cabin, Dave."

Kerchival nodded. "I had that figured. It was Tully, of course, figuring I had the will on me. When I didn't, Tully knew it would be in Mel Rhodes's safe. Go on, Deaf."

Deaf took another drag at his cup. "Well, then there was talk of a row because Hendron wouldn't pay for the will without you to go along with it, Dave. He figgered, I guess, it still wouldn't mean anything with you runnin' loose. So then Tully set out to collect you. He told Hendron he had you, safe and ready for delivery. But still Hendron balked, sayin' he wasn't interested in anything any more. So then Tully set to gibin' him about Lear and Virg, sayin' that he'd see they heard the whole story, from beginnin' to end, unless Hendron just about handed everything he owned over to him. That was when Hendron musta gone for his gun. Anyway, there was two shots. I come alive then an' yelled an' started bangin' on the door. Tully put out the light an' ducked out through the house the back way. I never did see him again. I finally got sense enough to open the door like it was made to be opened and got a light goin'. There was Abel Hendron, huddled in his chair and plenty dead. His gun was layin' on the floor beside him, but he hadn't got off a shot. Tully had got there first. And that, I reckon, is the story."

"Just about all," put in Dusty. "Joe, here, says that Turk Ballard is laid up over at War Hatchet with a smashed-up arm. Joe was there when they brought Turk in and went to town after Doc Cable."

"Hendron knew about Spence and Gard Ballard, too, by that time," said Joe Orchard. "He looked like a man who'd had some vital part of him yanked plumb out and thrown away."

Dave Kerchival nodded somberly. "He was beginning to re-alize then all that he'd torn down in trying to build his crazy dream. His own kids . . . his nephews. We saw the Ballards as being no good, but to Hendron they were his nephews. I can see now why he wouldn't deal with Tully. There wasn't anything that meant a damn to him any more. No matter what Tully might have been able to bring to him, he'd lost all the things that counted. Must be hell to see everything straight after it's too late to do any good about it."

"Wish I'd been with you to take care of Tully, Dave," Joe Orchard said. "That was my rightful job."

Kerchival agreed: "I know, Joe. I thought about that when I was heading back to his hide-out camp, but there wasn't time to locate you and take you along. For I knew, if Tully beat me back and found me gone, he'd have spooked and headed far and wide, and we might never have caught up with him. As it was, I didn't beat him there by much."

"Sure," said Joe. "I understand. There's one mean job left. That's tellin' Lear about her father . . . that he's gone. Bound to hurt her, plenty. And I guess I'm elected."

"Yes, you are," said Kerchival. He looked around. "There's just us that's here that know the truth about all of Abel Hen-dron's past. And I want the word of all of you that here is where it stays. Lear is no fool and, for that matter, neither is Virg. They may wonder and they may guess. But they're never to know all of it from any of us. All we know is that Jack Tully killed Abel Hendron because of some private squabble of their own. And that score has been evened. Everybody understand?"

"Sure," said Dusty Elliot gruffly. "Sure we do, Dave. The real story dies right here."

Joe Orchard asked: "How about Bill Yeager's will, Dave?"

Kerchival tapped a pocket. "I've got it. Tully had it on him. I don't know as I want it any more. The damned thing has cost too much."

"That's not the way to look at it," said Joe Orchard quietly. "It came to you clean, with a good man's right thinking behind it. Hang onto it. Right now you're thinking down dark trails. Give time a chance to work. A month from now you'll feel different. Well, now I got to head for town and face Lear Hendron . . . and hurt her. And I'd rather take a horsewhipping." He went to the door, paused there. "I'm a hell of a deputy sheriff. I ran myself ragged chasing blind trails an' never did show up in time where it counted. But they can't say I didn't try."

He went out, leaving a momentary silence, which Perk O'Dair finally broke with a soft murmur: "Joe can still pack the star for my money."

Chapter Twenty-Two

There was plenty to do, which was a godsend to Dave Kerchival. For the next ten days he virtually lived in the saddle. There was a grisly chore to be done at Lazy Y and another at War Hatchet. Jack Tully and Spence and Gard Ballard went back to the earth and the earth did not complain. Across the ages saint or sinner did not matter. Virg Hendron came out to War Hatchet with Joe Orchard and took care of Abel Hendron, the body going into Warm Creek for burial. Virg was grim and quiet, a little older and much wiser.

Dave Kerchival and his crew of Dusty and Perk and Chick went down to join Brace Shotwell and the plains riders in the chore of rounding up the scattered herd, bunching it, and starting it once more on the drive past the Mount Cherokee rim. This time the trail was open.

The long, action-filled days were cleansing to mind and soul, and at night, drugged with the fatigue of long hours of toil, a man could know the peace of deep sleep. The lines began to leave Dave Kerchival's face and the gleam of normalcy came back into his eyes. He found that Joe Orchard's prophecy was a sound one. Time was the great curative.

The cattle drive done with, the new bunkhouse was completely finished, and other odds and ends about Lazy Y headquarters cleaned up. Then Kerchival started on a range count of his own cattle. This was barely done with when one day Virg Hendron rode in. Virg was quiet, grave, steady-eyed, and seemed to know exactly what he wanted.

"Lear and I've gone home," he told Kerchival. "Don't suppose I left you with any memories to recommend me, Dave, but I want you to know that things will be different from here on out. Unless you're going to keep 'em for good, I'd like some of the old hands back."

"Glad you brought that up, Virg," said Kerchival heartily. "This spread ain't big enough to pack a three-man crew beside myself. The boys know it, too. I'm sure Perk and Chick will be glad to stow war bags at War Hatchet again, and I know Deaf is lonesome for his old kitchen. I'll keep Dusty. We hit it off pretty well, him and me. Is that fair?"

"Plenty. I couldn't ask for more. If you should get stuck for extra help any time, just holler and we'll come a-running. What I want to say is that, from now on, Kingfisher is just a creek, and not a line dividing anything any more."

Kerchival put out his hand. "I was never happier to shake on anything before in my life, Virg."

Kerchival got out the makings and rolled a smoke, then handed tobacco and papers across. Virg spun his smoke slowly. "There was a wrath visited on this range," he said gravely. "And somehow I got the feeling that mortal men didn't call all the turns. Me, I'm making no judgments and holding no grudges. Far as I'm concerned the slate is clean and it's a fresh start all around. Lear has been kind enough to call me brother again. That was everything to me and I'll never make her sorry." He hesitated slightly before going on. "About my father . . . there's a lot I'll never know and never want to know. But I'd like to feel that at the last he tried to clean the slate."

Kerchival picked his words carefully. "Your father died, Virg, trying a kill a human snake. That I know. I'd say that squared a lot of things."

Virg stared at his cigarette and nodded. "Thanks." He turned away, then paused to add a last remark. "Give Lear a little time, Dave."

The days turned and life fell into its measured grooves. Dave Kerchival made a trip out to Fort Devlin and filed the will for its legal probate process in Judge Archer's court. There was no question of its validity, and, when Kerchival returned to Warm Creek, it was with full knowledge that what Bill Yeager had wished to be, would be, without further question or doubt.

At Warm Creek, Kerchival dropped in at Joe Orchard's office. Joe was leaning back in his chair, smoking a cigar. Kerchival eyed him quizzically. "Going extravagant, eh? That rope must have cost all of a dime. What's the great occasion?"

Joe grinned. "Look me over and gaze upon a fellow cattleman."

"Shame on you," jeered Kerchival. "Been drinking, too."

"Sure," admitted Joe. "Hack Dinwiddie an' me had a couple to celebrate our partnership."

Kerchival pulled a chair around, straddled it, rested his crossed arms on the back. "Go ahead. I'm listening."

"The old Ballard layout," said Joe. "Hack an' me bought it. Turk Ballard, he's able to travel now, and he aims to, wanting no part of this range any more. Hack an' me talked it over, made him what we figgered was a fair offer for the layout, an' he grabbed it. I can see plenty arguments coming up between you an' me as to whose calf is which."

"I'll watch you and Hack like a hawk." Kerchival grinned. "Joe, that's great news. I've been wondering what we were going to do about Turk. I couldn't see much chance of him ever sweetening up. This sure provides an answer to that. But what are we going to do for a deputy sheriff?"

"Darned if I know, or care much," declared Joe. "I been livin' off the taxpayers long enough. And I doubt we're going to have much need of one from now on around here, Dave."

"I helped tear the old Ballard layout to pieces," Kerchival said. "So when you and Hack get ready to rebuild, just holler, and I'll be on hand to help with the chore."

"That's fair enough," agreed Joe. "Won't need much. Hack's going to stay on in town, running the hotel as usual. I'll be holding down the headquarters an' my needs will be simple."

They talked things over for a time, and then Kerchival left, making the rounds of town, dropping in here and there, getting the feel of old friendships again. There was no tension anywhere. Town was quiet, almost drowsy, and this was the way Kerchival liked it, a fixed and familiar landmark along a man's trail of life.

Coming up to Sam Liederman's store, his eyes darkened a little at sight of the familiar bench, standing beside the door. For a moment he was seeing again the man who used to sit on that bench a great deal and watch the flow of life along the street with pinched and unreadable eyes, a man who was twisted and dark and deadly inside. Well, that was something that was in the past now, along with a number of other things that time would smudge and finally obliterate entirely.

A tail thumped the store porch lazily and Kerchival bent to maul gently the ears of Sam Liederman's old Buster dog and make a little dog powwow. Then there was a light step and Kerchival looked up to see Lear Hendron standing in the doorway.

It was the first time he had seen her since the night when she'd come in to the hotel to live. Again he knew the old lift of feeling and he knew this was something that would never change. He had, he thought, never seen her looking better. At least not since the old days when they had danced together and knew on occasion the bright sound of her laughter. The haunted somberness was gone from her eyes and there was a relaxed softness about her mouth. She had the look of having found the earth's peacefulness again. She spoke simply.

"Hello, Dave."

She was dressed in riding togs and seemed about to leave town. Kerchival said: "If you're heading for home, Lear, I'd like to ride along."

"Of course," she said.

Kerchival got his horse from Bus Spurgeon's livery and they jogged out of town side-by-side, taking to the uplift of the slope trail. They moved into the timber and knew the richness of its resin-scented shadows. There was a silence between them that deepened and lengthened. Somehow Kerchival knew that this was the way Lear wanted it until she had thought out what she wanted to say. And finally she began to speak.

"There have been a lot of shadows, Dave, and there were many times when I thought they were so black and deep I'd never know what clear light was again. I was wrong. The human spirit, it seems, is tough and tenacious and demands to go on living. One's sense of values is flexible, and what seems enormously important from one point of view becomes totally unimportant when viewed from another angle. Time and events mold and change us. We learn to be content with what life sees fit to allow us to possess. And if we're smart, we shut the door firmly on the past and never open it again. How much can you forget about the Hendron family, Dave?"

"That's easy, Lear," he told her quietly. "All that needs to be forgotten. Yet that must work the other way, too. Past events didn't spare any of us. My part with the Ballards, for instance."

"I know," she said with a calm steadiness that surprised him. "Do you remember what I once said to you . . . that it was going to be terribly important to me to know that right could triumph? It did. So I will never be afraid of anything again as long as I live."

There was a scurry up the warm, brown trunk of a ponderosa pine beside them and a Douglas squirrel peered down with bright black eyes and jerked its tail and scolded them. Lear tipped her head and watched and smiled, and the line of her throat was as pure and clean as a reed curved before the wind.

"So the past is done," said Kerchival, watching her. "But what about the future . . . and us, Lear?"

She met his glance and held it, reading all there was in it. And nodded slowly, still smiling. "That was settled a long time ago, Dave."

It took considerable time and a deal of impatient scolding by the Douglas squirrel to get them, finally, to ride on, hand in hand.

ABOUT THE AUTHOR

L. P. Holmes was the author of a number of outstanding Western novels. Born in a snowed-in log cabin in the heart of the Rockies near Breckenridge, Colorado, Holmes moved with his family when very young to northern California and it was there that his father and older brothers built the ranch house where Holmes grew up and where, in later life, he would live again. He published his first story—"The Passing of the Ghost"—in *Action Stories* (9/25). He was paid 1/2¢ a word and received a check for $40. "Yeah . . . forty bucks," he said later. "Don't laugh. In those far-off days . . . a pair of young parents with a three-year-old son could buy a lot of groceries on forty bucks." He went on to contribute nearly six hundred stories of varying lengths to the magazine market as well as to write over fifty Western novels under his own name and the byline Matt Stuart. For many years of his life, Holmes would write in the mornings and spend his afternoons calling on a group of friends in town, among them the blind Western author, Charles H. Snow, who Lew Holmes always called Judge Snow (because he was Napa's Justice of the Peace in 1920–1924) and who frequently makes an appearance in later novels as a local justice in Holmes's imaginary Western communities. Holmes produced such notable novels as *Somewhere They Die* (1955) for which he received the Spur Award from the Western Writers of America. *Desert Steel* (Five Star, 2011) marked his most recent appearance. In these novels one finds the themes so basic to his

Western fiction: the loyalty that unites one man to another, the pride one must take in his work and a job well done, the innate generosity of most of the people who live in Holmes's ambient Western communities, and the vital relationship between a man and a woman in making a better life. His next Five Star Western will be *Once in the Saddle*.